Amelia's Dream

A Colonial Girl's Adventures

D1496426

Jami Borek

Amelia's Dream

ISBN-10   0991536657
ISBN-13   978-0-9915366-5-8

Published by:

Shrewsbury
Press

chapter 1

Amelia had shelled so many beans that her fingers could do it almost automatically. As her fingers pulled the beans out of their shells and dropped them into the wooden bowl on her lap, her mind couldn't help but wander.

First she was wondering what to buy at the Fredericksburg Market Fair. The Fair was only a couple of weeks away now. Some sweetmeats of course, but what kind? Lemon drops? Sugared almonds? What about a new silken ribbon for her cap? Did she have enough money for a new pair of earrings?

Then her thoughts turned to years away, thinking about the far-off future. Someday, when she was grown up, she'd be leaving the Browns. She would have to be on her own then. She didn't want to be a servant all her life, but what else could she do? What would she do to support herself?

All the time Amelia was shelling beans, Miss Elizabeth had been busy cooking dinner at the fireplace. She stirred the soup in the heavy iron stew pot that hung over the fire and turned and basted the roast on the long iron spit that hung there also. Then she straightened up, massaged her back, and turned to look at Amelia. When she saw Amelia still wasn't done, she gave her the most terrible frown.

"You haven't finished yet?" she said angrily. "I swear, you're the slowest girl I ever did know. Hurry up! I need to get them cooking."

Miss Elizabeth could be a strict old sourpuss, like she was now, but Amelia knew that the cook really liked her. She always made sure that Amelia had plenty to eat and even gave her special treats in addition. Sometimes it might be an extra baked apple with whipped sweet cream or an extra-large slice of sweet potato pie. Sometimes, if Amelia was lucky, it was her very favorite treat—bits of leftover dough fried in butter and sprinkled with cinnamon and sugar.

Amelia knew that her life was pretty good, all things considered. Miss Elizabeth was nice to her and so were Mr. and Mrs. Brown, the couple she worked for.

The Browns treated Amelia pretty well, especially considering that they didn't have so much themselves to begin with. They weren't even well-to-do, much less wealthy. All their lives they'd worked here and there, in different places around Virginia. They did whatever they could for whoever would hire them. Now they lived in Fredericksburg, helping with Mr. Dixon's store and living in a house that he'd lent them.

Mr. Dixon didn't charge them any rent at all. He owned a lot of houses in Fredericksburg and a lot of them were empty. Amelia had heard Mr. Brown talking about it to Mrs. Brown. Mr. Dixon thought Fredericksburg was growing so fast that he could make money selling houses, so he'd borrowed a lot of money to buy and build them.

"The man's a dreamer," Mr. Brown had said, sounding worried and disapproving. "Who's going to buy all these houses? Now he's in debt and how will he get out of it? The town's not growing so fast as that. Where are all the rich folks going to come from, that can afford to buy all those houses?"

The Browns weren't in debt and that was a blessing, but they didn't have much money either. They lived pretty much from day to day, with nothing left over for saving.

Still they gave Amelia what they could, and even some little luxuries. She had warm clothes for the winter and plenty of food. She had a nice cozy mattress to sleep on, with a soft feather pillow and a real wool blanket. They even gave her a pair of leather shoes with shiny brass buckles and little silver rings for her earlobes.

Sometimes they would yell at her and scold her, but mostly when they did, she knew she'd done something foolish. Like the time she'd gotten angry at a customer in the store and told him that he was stupid. She'd gotten in a lot of trouble over that but she understood why. You couldn't expect the customers to come back to your store if you called them names. There were other stores they could go to.

The Browns didn't have many servants, just Amelia and Miss Elizabeth. So Amelia helped Miss Elizabeth in the kitchen and did all kinds of other chores. She laid the wood for the fires, lit them, and tended them to keep them burning nicely. She did the washing up and the cleaning, helped with the laundry and the store, and ran errands whenever they asked her to.

Once she'd finished shelling the beans ("It's about time you finished, you lazy girl!" Miss Elizabeth said to her crossly), Amelia watched over the food while it finished cooking. She stirred the pot, turned the roast, and added more wood to keep the fire nicely burning. Then, when the roast was done and Miss Elizabeth took it off the spit to carve, Amelia set the table.

She laid out the knives, plates, and spoons, lining them up neatly on the bare wood table. There were just two of everything, one for Mr. Brown and one for his wife. Miss Elizabeth and Amelia didn't eat with them. They usually ate the leftovers when the Browns were done, sitting there on stools in the kitchen.

Amelia wondered what it would be like to eat dinner at a proper table every day, not with the Browns, but with her very own parents. She couldn't really remember what it was like having parents. She was so young the last time she saw them. It was hard being all alone, with no mother, no father, no sisters, nor brothers. Sometimes she felt pretty lonely. She knew she was lucky though, compared to a lot of other people.

She just didn't know how lucky she was, not really. She didn't know it until later on, when all her good luck was gone.

chapter 2

The next day, Amelia and Mrs. Brown spent the morning in the store, unpacking new things that had just come in by ship from London. They'd been at it for hours now. The whole time, the rain had been pouring down so hard that there hadn't been any customers.

The heavy rain reminded Amanda of the flood they'd had just a few months before. It rained so hard and so long that the Rappahannock River turned into a raging, deadly wall of water. All along the river, warehouses and homes had been flooded, but that wasn't the worst of it. The river had destroyed everything in its path, even trees and ships and houses. It killed dozens of people, they said, or even hundreds.

All along the river, warehouses had been flooded

Thinking of the flood, Amelia felt frightened. She tried not to think about the rain and just pay attention to what she was doing.

Mrs. Brown carefully inspected and unpacked the crates and barrels, one by one. As she did, she checked each item off against the lists of what they'd ordered. Then Amelia shelved and arranged things around the store. Unpacking and arranging things was hard work, but Amelia and Mrs. Brown were happy to be doing it. They were pleased to see the store filling up with goods again. For so long now, the shelves had been almost empty.

Two years ago, a group of important Virginians, including George Washington, had decided there should be a boycott. That is, no one would buy certain kinds of things from Britain, where almost everything came from.

The boycott was a way of protesting the taxes that the British Parliament was making them pay, but the real problem wasn't really the taxes. The taxes weren't very high and people could generally afford them. The problem was that the Parliament was forcing them to do things and they didn't have any say in it.

The Parliament wasn't treating them like proper Englishmen, that's what people said. Virginians were supposed to have same rights as people living in Britain. Instead they were being treated like servants, or even worse. The Parliament seemed to think colonists were people you could just order around and treat as badly as you liked. Even the King seemed to think so.

So many things had to come from Britain that nearly everyone gave up something for the boycott. It covered tea and wine, and lots of other foods, like beef, pork, fish, barley, fruit, pickles, butter, cheese, and sugar. Furniture and watches were prohibited too, along with jewelry, ribbons, lace, fabrics, shoes, candles, looking glasses, and things made of leather, gold, and silver.

It wasn't just the Virginians who were upset about the taxes. Other colonies were unhappy too and there were other complaints and boycotts. Finally, the protests worked and the British Parliament repealed most of the taxes. They did keep the tax on tea, however, just to show they could do it.

In July, George Washington and the others had decided to end the boycott in Virginia. Now the wooden ships with their great canvas sails were coming to Fredericksburg again. They sailed from England and from the British Caribbean Islands, across the ocean and up the Rappahannock River, bringing all the things they'd been missing.

After they'd been working non-stop all morning, Mrs. Brown finally decided it was time to take a break. She asked Amelia to brew her a cup of tea.

"Brew two cups," she told Amelia. "You've been working so hard, you can have one too."

Amelia didn't even like tea all that much (she only drank it with loads of milk and sugar) but she was pleased. It was a big treat anyway. With the boycott, tea had become as rare as rubies. Even now, there was still a boycott on buying tea, since the Parliament had kept the tea tax.

Mrs. Brown had only a small, secret supply of tea that she'd saved from before the boycott. She kept it locked away in a small wooden box and she was the only one with the key. She hardly ever shared it.

They sat there quietly for a little while, sipping their tea, listening to the rain still pouring down and looking around the store to see how much they'd accomplished.

"Tell me again, how was it I came to be here with you?" Amelia asked, after a few minutes of sitting there in silence.

Mrs. Brown sighed.

"Not again! I've told you that so many times, the words are just about worn out."

"Once more, please?" Amelia pleaded.

Amelia knew that Mrs. Brown was tired of telling the story over and over again, but she couldn't help asking. When Mrs. Brown repeated the story, Amelia seemed to remember it all, as if it had happened just a little while before, instead of so long ago.

Did she really remember? Amelia was never really sure. Maybe it was just her imagination, making up pictures to go with whatever Mrs. Brown was saying. Still it was so important to her, either way. It was nice to have some memories.

She had so little else to remember her parents by, hardly anything. Just one keepsake, a small heart-shaped locket with a bit of her mother's hair inside.

That was all she had. There were no portraits (they were too poor for that), no letters, no other jewelry. Amelia didn't even know anyone who could tell her about her parents or her life before—no other family, no neighbors, no one who'd known them.

"Please tell me?" Amelia begged again. She knew that if she kept asking, Mrs. Brown would give in eventually.

Mrs. Brown knew it too, and she also knew that Amelia would keep on asking and asking.

Mrs. Brown put down her teacup.

"All right," she gave in reluctantly and then began. "It all started once upon a time . . . ."

She always started the very same way, "once upon a time." As if it was a fairy-tale that she'd read somewhere, instead of something that had actually happened.

"I heard it was summer," Mrs. Brown continued, "and you were very young."

Yes, it must have been summer. Amelia really did think she remembered. She remembered the feeling of the air, so thick and heavy with humidity and heat.

It was the time when the fevers came and her mother got the fever. One day she was there, lying in bed and stroking Amelia's hair. Soon after, there was her funeral.

"So your mother died," Mrs. Brown was saying. Amelia had missed some of what she'd said, being lost in her own memories, but it didn't matter. She knew how the story went so well, she could recite it by heart. "They say your father was a sailor. Most of the time, he was gone off sailing. So the church vestrymen and the Court took charge, since he couldn't be around to take care of you."

"That was in Williamsburg, yes?"

"Yes, Williamsburg," Mrs. Brown agreed.

Amelia thought she remembered it. The court was full of people, sitting there on row after row of wooden benches. All the benches faced a sort of raised up platform in the back of the room, with a wooden railing all around and a desk on the floor in front of it.

Then a gentleman came and sat at the desk (he was called the clerk, they told her later), and the Justices came in and seated themselves on the platform. They all wore the same white wigs and they all looked very solemn. Even then, as young as she was and not understanding what was going on, Amelia knew these men were very important.

"That's where you were living then, so it was the Williamsburg court that bound you out. That's how it happened."

"*Bound out.*" For a long time, Amelia was too young to know what it meant. Mrs. Brown had explained it to her when she was older. It was what they did with orphans, she said, giving them to someone else to raise. It was sort of like being an apprentice or an indentured servant. The orphans were bound out to work for someone else for so

They faced a raised up platform
with a desk in front of it

many years, and they raised you and taught you skills so you could be on your own when you were old enough.

It was the church that was responsible for taking care of the orphans and poor in the parish, but it was the Court that made it all legal and binding. So they went to the Court, her father and her sister too. That day was the last time she ever saw them.

"A sister?" she'd asked eagerly, the first time Mrs. Brown had told the story. "I have a sister? Where is she now? Is she older or younger?"

"I don't know, I'm afraid," Mrs. Brown had said in reply, sad to see Amelia was so very disappointed. "I can only tell you what we were told by Mr. Waller, the Clerk of the Court in Williamsburg. We weren't there, Mr. Brown and I, when it all happened. You were bound out to a tailor then, but that didn't work out—I don't know why—so you ended up with us. We were in Williamsburg then, but not too much later we moved to Fredericksburg."

"And if something happens, so that it doesn't work out with you, could it happen again?" Amelia had asked worriedly. "Could I be taken away from you and given to someone else altogether?"

"Now don't you go on worrying about things that haven't happened yet," Mrs. Brown had answered quickly with a little frown. The way she said it, Amelia knew the answer to her question was "yes." It could happen.

Someday, somehow, she could be taken away from the Browns and given to someone else. They might not be anywhere near as nice as the Browns and she wouldn't have any say in it. Sometimes, when she was in a worrying mood, it was something Amelia worried about. But she didn't worry all that hard. If she'd known what was to come, she'd have worried very much harder.

chapter 3

Soon enough though, there was something else to worry about. Mrs. Brown fell down the stairs one night and broke her arm, because it was dark and she was hurrying. It was a big problem for everyone in the house, especially for Mrs. Brown herself. It was her right arm that she broke and she was right-handed.

Doctor Mercer came to the house the next morning to set the bones and fit her with a brace to hold it straight. Then he bled her too—"just for good measure" is how he put it.

Amelia had seen bleeding before, but she'd always tried not to look at it. This time her curiosity was stronger than the upset feeling in her stomach. When he bled Mrs. Brown, Amelia made herself pay especially close attention.

Doctor Mercer took Mrs. Brown's arm, laid it out straight, and raised up the vein by tapping on it. Then he made a little nick with a sharp little blade called a lancet, straight across the vein.

"This takes training," he warned Amelia very seriously. "It has to be done just right. Otherwise, it can be deadly dangerous. Never even think of trying this on yourself or anyone. If you do it even a little bit wrong, you could bleed to death."

Doctor Mercer let the vein bleed until the bleeding bowl was as full as he thought it ought to be. Then he put a compress on Mrs. Brown's arm and made her hold it tight to stop any more bleeding. He took the bowl of blood over to the window so he could inspect it in good light and looked at it very closely.

"Doctors can tell a lot by looking at the blood," he told Amelia. "See this?" He held the bowl up close to her face so she could inspect it carefully. "It's nice and red, isn't it?"

Looking at the bowl of blood up close, Amelia was definitely getting a queasy feeling in her stomach. She tried to ignore it and see if she could see what he was talking about. Yes, she thought, it's a very bright red. Like her own blood, when she pricked her finger with a needle sewing.

"That's a good sign, being red like that," Doctor Mercer told her once she'd taken a really good look at it. "When a person has a fever it gets what we call 'sizey'—kind of a white crust on the top of it. That's a sure sign of inflammation."

So that was how she first got to know Doctor Mercer.

Afterwards, while Mrs. Brown was healing, Amelia went to his shop quite often for ointment and pills and bandages. The shop was full of so many curious things that Amelia kept pestering him with questions.

There were shelves and shelves full of green glass jars and white glass jars and pots made of blue-and-white china. Each of them held some different kind of herb or potion and they were all very neatly labeled. Some were things she knew, like "Cinnamon" and "Lavender," but others had wonderful, exotic names like "Flowers of Sulfur," "Dragon's Blood," and "Brimstone."

In addition to herbs and potions, Doctor Mercer also had many different kinds of medical equipment. There were mortars and pestles of different sizes, some made of granite and some of marble and some of pottery. There were forceps and saws and other instruments that Amelia had never seen before. Some of them looked very strange and terrible.

The strangest thing of all, to Amelia's mind, was the leeches. They were right there on a table by where Doctor Mercer did the surgery, in glass jars full of water. The leeches were used for bleeding sometimes, instead of the little knives. You'd just put them on the arm and they'd

latch on and suck the blood. For leeches, blood was their dinner.

Doctor Mercer had to feed them animal blood, he said, if they didn't get enough from his bleeding people.

Amelia had been bled by leeches before, though she'd always tried not to think about it. The funny thing was, it didn't hurt. When they bit into your arm, you didn't even feel it.

Doctor Mercer never minded answering her questions. He appreciated having an audience. He began to wonder though, was this young girl really interested in a serious way or was it just idle curiosity? So one day, he decided to test her. The next time she came in, he was busy grinding up something with a mortar and pestle, but he stopped what he was doing and started asking her questions.

"Here's the Peruvian bark," he began, pulling down one of the blue and white china jars. "Some call it Jesuit's bark. Do you remember what it's good for?"

"For the fevers," Amelia answered right away, "especially the fevers that come and go and come again, with cold and then sweating. It's called—" she hesitated, trying to concentrate. "It's called 'the ague and fever' or also 'the intermittent fever'," she went on, remembering. "You can get it from the dismal swamp air. It's best to take the bark in a powder form, dissolved in liquid."

She looked at Doctor Mercer anxiously to see if she'd answered correctly.

"Yes, that's right," he nodded. Then he thought, maybe his question had been too easy. It was only a couple of days ago that he'd talked about the Peruvian bark. He pulled down another jar and held it out so she could see the label. "What about this one?"

"Allium, or garlic, is good for bites and poisons," she answered. "It's hot and dry in nature, so it's good for the bites of cold beasts especially, like snakes and toads and spiders."

Doctor Mercer nodded his approval.

"That's right."

Yes, it was exactly what he'd told her. The girl had a good memory, he'd give her that. But how good was she really? Maybe she'd just been lucky. Maybe he'd just happened to pick out things she remembered. So he asked her about something from the week before and then the week before that.

It quickly became sort of a game, him going round the shop and pointing out this and that and asking her what it was. Nearly every time she answered him correctly.

He was busy grinding up something

"You've remembered nearly every word I said," he concluded finally. "That's pretty impressive, I have to say. Why are you so interested?"

"I've decided that I want to be a doctor when I grow up," she answered simply. She'd never really realized it before Mrs. Brown broke her arm, but then it came to her very suddenly. It was very clear, as if that was always what she'd wanted to do and she'd always known it.

"I'm afraid that's impossible, my dear." Doctor Mercer looked at her sympathetically, but he sounded very certain. "Only men can be doctors. You can be a nurse or a midwife, or a mother who takes care of her family. But only men are doctors."

"But what about Mrs. Livingston?" Amelia asked reasonably. "She was a doctor. She was practicing here in Fredericksburg for years and years. Lots of people went to be treated by her."

Doctor Mercer looked a bit surprised at first but then he thought about it.

"Well, I guess that's so," he said, "but that was a different situation. Her husband was a doctor and then he died. She was his widow. Widows often continue their husbands' trades, like Mrs. Gordon's taking over the tavern when her husband died. So I guess if you want to be a doctor, you ought to marry one."

He smiled a bit at that, but it made Amelia angry.

"But if a woman can do it after her husband dies, why can't she do it beforehand? What does it matter if her husband is dead or alive—or if she's even married?"

Doctor Mercer thought and thought, but he couldn't come up with an answer.

"I don't know," he confessed at last. "There's something to what you say, but that's how it is. That's how it's always been. If you want to be a doctor, then you'd better marry one."

Amelia felt sad at that. Underneath the sadness, though, she felt stubborn. If Mrs. Livingston could do it, there had to be a way. Just because it had always been a certain way, didn't mean it couldn't be different in the future.

Then she had a troubling thought.

"Does that mean you won't teach me anymore?" she asked him anxiously.

She looked so very serious and worried that Doctor Mercer felt sorry for her. He smiled at her reassuringly.

"No, that's all right my dear. I'll teach you anyway, if you're that interested. You won't be able to call yourself an apothecary or a doctor, but you can still do medicine. I can't spend all my time answering your questions, though," he added. "I've got my shop and my practice to tend to. How about if I lend you a book to read? Can you read? Would you take good care of it?"

"Oh, yes!" Amelia said excitedly.

He disappeared into the back and came out with a thick, heavy-looking book bound in leather.

"This is Doctor Buchan's *Domestic Medicine*," he said, handing it over to her. "It will tell you about the different diseases and how to cure them."

"Thank you!" Amelia took it excitedly and opened it up, glancing through some of the pages.

As excited as she was, she was also a bit dismayed, though she tried not to show it.

Mrs. Brown had taught her to read but her teaching was very basic. She didn't think girls needed to read very much (she didn't herself), just useful practical things like receipts and  recipes, to help with the shop and the cooking.

Now here was this book more than six hundred pages long, with so many complicated words and even some words that looked like Latin. It was a wonderful book, full of so many things she wanted to know. The only problem was, could she read it?

chapter 4

Luckily, *Domestic Medicine* was easier to read than she'd feared. Luckily also, Doctor Mercer didn't mind answering her questions. Whenever she didn't understand some part or didn't know some particular word, she'd make a list and the next time she saw him, she'd ask him and he would answer.

Luckiest of all, Mrs. Brown didn't mind her taking time to read it. Though, as she told Amelia often enough, she thought Amelia was crazy to waste so much of her time on it.

Mrs. Brown was kind that way. She made sure that Amelia wasn't overloaded with chores, so Amelia usually had time for some fun things also. Mrs. Brown even let her skip some of her chores when there was something extra special going on, like the Fredericksburg Fair.

The Fair was held twice a year, once toward the end of May and then again toward the end of September. The Fairs were the highlight of the entire year. They were more festive even than Christmas. The main purpose of the Fair was for people to get together to buy and sell things, but that was only part of it. During the Fair, people streamed into Fredericksburg from all around and the town was full of excitement.

With so many different people coming to town at the same time, it became a sort of very large party. Wandering musicians played up and down the streets, some with fiddles and others with flutes or penny whistles. There were horse races, plays, and concerts. You could see friends you hadn't seen since the fair before, taste special foods, and enjoy the special entertainments.

Amelia could hardly wait for the September Fair. She'd been thinking about it for weeks now. She didn't have much money to spend, so she'd thought long and hard what she might purchase. She decided that she could afford some sweetmeats and a nice new silk ribbon, most likely a pink one. She'd also saved up whatever she could, hoping she could afford to buy a new pair of earrings.

She also really wanted to see a play. She'd never seen a real live play before and this time the American Company was performing. She'd heard about them, everyone had. They were famous actors and actresses and they were coming to Fredericksburg!

She'd begged Mrs. Brown to let her go but Mrs. Brown wouldn't even consider it. She said the plays they were putting on, "The Provoked Husband" and "Love à la Mode," weren't suitable for a girl as young as she was.

"Maybe next time," Mrs. Brown had said to make her feel better. "I hear that sometime later on they'll be performing *Romeo and Juliet*. I suppose that would be all right since it's written by Mr. Shakespeare."

Amelia was disappointed, but not for very long. Mrs. Brown gave her the whole day off and an extra five pence to spend to make up for it. Now she could definitely afford those earrings!

"You watch out now," Mrs. Brown called after her as she left the house. "There's all kinds of people in town for the Fair, including pickpockets, thieves, and other criminals. Wanted men, some of them! During the Fair, they can come to town without fear of being arrested."

"Yes, Mrs. Brown." Amelia automatically agreed, but she wasn't really paying attention.

She spent the entire morning just wandering around town. Since it was the harvest season, the goods for sale were plentiful. There were rosy red apples, cabbages, pumpkins, corn, squash, and greens. There were chestnuts, walnuts, wool, beeswax candles, and honey. There were lots of dried herbs, cheese and cider, and livestock too, pigs, cows, sheep, guinea fowl, and chickens.

Amelia bought some bread and cheese and nibbled on it as she wandered around. She spent an especially long time looking at all the horses. These were the very best and fastest horses you could find, because one of the most popular entertainments during the Fair was the horse racing. Every gentleman for miles around who had horses that could race, had one horse that he was particularly proud of. So he brought that horse to town to race at the Fair, to see if his horse was faster than the others.

After giving the matter considerable thought, Amelia picked out one horse as her favorite. It was a beautiful white stallion, quietly feeding in a fenced-in field behind one of the houses.

She spent a few precious coins on an apple at one of the stalls. Then she went up to the fence and held the apple out in her hand, very cautiously. When the stallion perked up his head and started coming her way, she suddenly got a bit worried. What if he was greedy and bit her hand? But he gave her a soft whinny, as if to say "don't be afraid," and then he nibbled the apple right out of her hand. He took it ever so gently.

After that, she was hungry again herself, so she bought a little paper parcel of lemon drops from the seller of sweet-meats. She bought a lovely pink ribbon to tie around her cap and then it was time for the slack rope walker's performance.

"What's a slack rope walker?" she'd asked Mrs. Brown, when she heard one was coming.

"Do you know what a tight rope walker is?" Mrs. Brown had asked her back.

"Yes, I guess so," Amelia had said hesitantly. "That's someone who walks on a tight rope strung between two trees or something, isn't it?"

"Well, a slack rope walker is just the same, only the rope isn't tight, it's loose. So the rope can move around more. In some ways it's even harder."

When Amelia got to where the slack rope walker was performing, she was surprised to see that it was a woman. "Signora La Rosa" (for that, she said, was her name), was a sight to see, dressed in a big white shirt, a bright red lace-up bodice, and gigantic short pantaloons striped in black and yellow.

When Amelia got there, Signora La Rosa was standing by her rope and telling the crowd that her show would be truly amazing.

"You must shout 'Bravo!'" she said, "to show you are pleased! You must applaud most enthusiastically!"

Amelia looked at the rope. It was big and thick, and tied at the ends to two wooden stands to hold it. It hung only a little ways off the ground, not stretched tight but hanging fairly loosely.

"That's not so hard," Amelia thought to herself when she saw the rope. "I could walk on that myself, I think, with a little practice."

She changed her mind, however, when Signora La Rosa started performing. It wasn't just a matter of standing on the rope, though that was harder than it looked, Amelia quickly realized. In addition, the slack rope walker did amazing tricks while she was balancing on the rope, and all the time she was moving along the rope, forward and even backward.

Signora La Rosa started out with easier things, like walking back and forth while playing a flute and then

Walking back and forth
while holding a parasol

while holding a big paper parasol. As she went on, the tricks got harder and harder. All the while she was calling out to the crowd, saying things that were so funny that everyone was laughing.

Then she juggled different kinds of objects while standing on a big red ball and balancing very carefully. First she juggled little white balls—three balls, then four, then five, and then six balls! She got one of the audience to throw them to her.

Next she juggled three very long, sharp knives. First it was only three, but then it was four, and then five of them. It looked so dangerous, like any moment she'd slip and cut off her hand, that Amelia was almost afraid to watch her.

Just as Signora La Rosa had asked, the audience clapped and clapped and shouted "Bravo!" most enthusiastically. It was such a loud and cheerful noise that more and more people came over to watch her.

Soon the crowd was so thick that people trying to pass by could hardly get past it. Most people took the long way around but some of the ruder and bolder sort simply pushed their way through, shoving with their shoulders and hips and elbows.

Toward the end of the show, someone shoved into Amelia so hard they almost knocked her down. She would have fallen, in fact, but someone behind her grabbed onto her waist and held her upright.

Then, at the very end, came the trick that was most spectacular. Signora La Rosa set three torches on fire and juggled them too, with one end to catch and the other end burning. And all the time she was traveling back and forth on the wiggly rope, without even looking where she was walking.

When the show was over, Signora La Rosa was passing a basket around for the audience to give her money. So Amelia reached into her pocket to give her a coin, but her pocket seemed emptier than it should be.

Feeling around inside, she finally found a few pence, but there didn't seem to be as many coins left as there ought to be. What had happened to the money for her earrings?!

Anxiously her fingers explored the entire inside of her pocket. The bottom was sound and snug, there wasn't any tear or hole, but something was definitely missing. With a growing fear, she untied it from around her waist and carefully took out everything inside. It was empty except for a few small coins and a single lemon drop.

All the rest of her money was gone, and her silken ribbon too, but that wasn't the worst thing. What was very much worse, was that she was missing the little bag that held her locket. Her mother's locket, it was gone! Her one great treasure, her only keepsake!

As tears formed in her eyes, Amelia suddenly remembered how someone had shoved her so hard when she was watching Signora La Rosa. Then someone else grabbed her to hold her up. That's what she'd thought at the time, anyway. But maybe it wasn't someone being nice at all? Maybe he'd also reached inside her pocket?

Maybe the other one, the one who shoved her—maybe he did it on purpose? Were they working together, one to run into some-

Her pocket was empty!

one like that and the other one to pick their pocket while pretending to help them?

Mrs. Brown had warned her there might be pickpockets. If only she'd paid more attention!

While such thoughts whirled through her mind, tears were running down her cheeks. Her heart felt like it was breaking. Her locket, it was gone! She'd lost the only thing she had to remember her mother by!

Dazed, she made her way to the edge of the square and desperately searched the crowd. What did they look like, the pickpockets? It had all happened so fast, she could hardly remember. Of course they'd be gone by now, gone for good. Gone away with her locket.

Amelia was so shaken by the loss, so sad and hopeless that she felt dizzy. She looked around for somewhere she could sit down to try to recover. Then she felt someone tugging at her sleeve and she quickly jerked around. Not again—not another pickpocket!

But no, there was just a young boy. He smiled when she turned and saw him. Then he reached in his own pocket and held something out to her.

"Here," he said proudly, "I'm thinking these belong to you."

He was holding out her little bag, some coins, and her silken ribbon.

Slowly she reached out to take her things with a trembling hand, half hopeful and half fearful. Her little bag! Was the locket still in it? When she felt the bag in her hand, her heart leapt with joy. Yes, there was something still inside. She opened it and looked in. Yes, there was her locket!

After that of course, nothing would do but to take the boy back to the shop, give him a bag of their finest peppermints, and listen to his story.

"I saw this man run into you," young Jacob recounted (for that was his name), "and the other one dip his hand in your pocket, when he was pretending to help you. It didn't seem fair to me, two mean old fellows like that and you just a poor young girl, so I followed them. It wasn't hard. I'm short and I'm little, so I could slip through the crowd and they never even noticed me."

"But how did you get it back? Surely they didn't drop it?"

Jacob gave her a look, as if she'd said something very silly.

"They took it from you, so I took it back from them, didn't I?"

He saw that she didn't understand it still, so he showed her. He wiggled his fingers, and then pretended to reach into a man's pocket and pull something out.

"I'm as good as they is, even better. My hands is smaller and I've been practicing."

"You stole it?" She was shocked and disbelieving. "You're practicing to be a pickpocket too?"

"Oh no, nothing like that." He said it a bit too quickly. "I'm only playing around. For fun." He smiled, but he wouldn't look her in the eyes. He didn't sound very convincing.

She didn't know what to say, but she didn't have to.

"I have to go now," Jacob said quickly. He was out the door before she knew it. "Be more careful next time," he called back over his shoulder, "and thanks for the peppermints!"

chapter 5

Not very long after the Fair, just a couple of days or so, Amelia went again to see Doctor Mercer. It was Miss Elizabeth the cook who sent her this time, to get her some of a patent medicine called Daffy's Elixir.

As Amelia approached the shop, she could hear the doctor shouting. His voice was so loud that she could hear it right out there in the street, even though the windows were shut and the thick, heavy door was closed tightly.

"You're a thief!" she heard him shout. "I'll have the Sheriff on you. You'll be whipped and locked in the pillory!"

Afraid to go in, Amelia peeked in the window. She saw a young boy struggling to free himself from Doctor

Mercer's grip. The boy looked familiar. Was it someone she knew? Then she suddenly realized it was Jacob!

She couldn't help but go in then, to see what the matter was.

When Jacob saw Amelia, he suddenly stopped struggling and just stood there. All his spirit was gone. He looked sheepish and sad and as pitiful as anything.

"What's the matter?" Amelia asked Doctor Mercer timidly. "What has he done?"

"This little thief, this ruffian?" Doctor Mercer said angrily. "He tried to steal some Peruvian bark, is what he did. Sneaking it out of a jar when my back was turned. A clever little thief he was, but I happened to turn around and caught him."

"Oh Jacob, how could you!" Amelia cried. It was more a statement than a question. She wasn't really surprised, remembering how he'd gotten her locket back and talked about practicing to be a pickpocket.

"It's for my sister, my baby sister." Jacob hung his head and he said it softly, pleading. "Her fever's so high and she's shaking so bad, I'm afraid she's going to die. I did it for my sister."

Amelia thought for a moment about how she would feel if she had a little sister who was dying. Then she reached in her pocket and pulled out some coins, all she had left of her savings.

"Please, Doctor Mercer," she said, holding out her tiny handful of coins, "will this pay for it? Please don't call the Sheriff. I'm sure he's learned his lesson."

Doctor Mercer looked at her with surprise.

"You know this thieving rascal?"

"Not really. But he did a wonderful thing for me the other day at the Fair. I was watching the slack rope walker and then someone bumped into me. Someone was picking my pocket, stealing the most important things ever in the world. Jacob saw them and he got my things back. I didn't even know him, but he saved me and he didn't even ask for a reward or anything."

Doctor Mercer looked from one to the other of them, considering. Jacob seemed a bright and kind-hearted boy—a little too kind-hearted, perhaps, if his affections were leading him into thievery.

"I think you'd better tell me about your baby sister," he said finally.

"She's the youngest, little Sally is, with a sweet little face like an angel." Jacob's face softened and, despite his predicament, he almost smiled. It was clear he was pretty fond of her. "She took sick about two weeks ago. At first we thought she'd get over it in a few days, like she did the time before. But she got worse and worse and it didn't go away, and she was getting weaker and weaker . . ."

His voice trailed off and his voice was rough with emotion. For the first time, Doctor Mercer's anger started to cool.

"It sounds pretty serious, I agree," he said gravely, "but that doesn't explain why you're stealing my medicine. Why aren't your parents taking care of her?"

"I don't know," Jacob said honestly. "They're just worn out, I guess, and they've given up hope for her. There's ten of us children at home. I'm number eight and then there's David, he's the ninth. And then there was Mary but she died. Sally was born a year or so ago and she's been sickly since the beginning. My mother's been sickly too, ever since Sally was born. Too many children and not enough money to keep them, that's what my father says."

Amelia was listening to all of this with keen attention. Ten children, and all still alive! That was pretty amazing. She felt awfully sorry for Jacob's mother, trying to take care of ten children and being sickly herself, doing all the chores and everything. No wonder Jacob was running around on his own and getting into so much trouble.

"I'll tell you what," Doctor Mercer said at last, "I'll go see your sister and your mother too. And in return you can work for me. You can clean the store, run errands, and take care of the fires. Maybe you can even roll some pills for me. It's a tricky thing to do well, but I imagine you can learn. You seem to be—" he glanced over at the medicine jar that Jacob had opened so quickly and silently and gave a sour little smile, "pretty good with your fingers."

chapter 6

Now that she had Jacob and Doctor Mercer as friends, Amelia thought that things were just about perfect. So long as she finished her chores, Mr. and Mrs. Brown didn't mind if she spent time studying *Domestic Medicine*, visiting the apothecary, or going to see Jacob and his family. So Amelia's life settled into a comfortable, pleasant routine. It would be just fine, she felt, if things stayed that way for ever.

In the mornings, Mr. and Mrs. Brown would sit in the parlor and talk about their plans for the day while they ate a simple breakfast. Amelia would bring them coffee (or sometimes tea from the secret supply) along with bread, cheese, and whatever was left over from yesterday's supper. Then, before she started on all her other chores, Amelia and Miss Elizabeth would eat a quick breakfast themselves in the kitchen.

It was a cheerful way to start the day. This morning though, as Amelia carried the tea-tray down the hall, Amelia sensed that something was wrong. She began to feel uneasy.

She could hear the Browns' voices through the parlor door. Mrs. Brown sounded pleading and sad. Mr. Brown sounded upset also. Amelia had heard them argue before, but somehow this was different. What could be wrong, to make them so unhappy?

Timidly, she knocked at the door. The conversation stopped. For a moment there was silence. Then Mr. Brown called out.

"Come in, Amelia."

Amelia entered the room, trying to act as if she hadn't heard anything unusual. Mr. Brown was sitting in his chair like he always did. Mrs. Brown was sitting at the desk with some papers spread out before her. Mr. Brown didn't look angry, not exactly. It was more like something bad was happening, that he wanted to fix but he couldn't.

Mrs. Brown gave Amelia a quick little look and then looked away at the desk in front of her. From the glimpse she'd had, Amelia could have sworn Mrs. Brown's eyes were red and puffy. It looked like she'd been crying, but

Mrs. Brown never cried, not once in all the time Amelia had been there.

Amelia carefully set the tray down on a table and handed Mr. Brown his coffee and Mrs. Brown her tea. It was a Souchong tea, from China, very dark and smoky.

Mr. Brown took his coffee but he didn't drink it. Mrs. Brown said softly that she didn't want any tea. No tea? To waste a cup of tea, already brewed and right there in the tea cup? Then Amelia knew right away that something really terrible must have happened.

She stood there, hoping they would say something to explain, but they just sat there in silence. Neither one of them looked at her and neither said a word.

"Is something wrong?" she asked finally. It wasn't really her place to ask but she couldn't help it.

Mr. Brown gave his wife a meaningful look.

"There, you see? You'd better tell her." With a sigh, he picked up his cup of coffee and left the room, leaving Mrs. Brown alone with Amelia.

After he left, there was another long moment of silence. Then Mrs. Brown looked away and sighed. It was a long, sad sigh.

"Business hasn't been so good lately," she began, and then she stopped and was silent.

Amelia was silent too, not knowing what to say.

"First the boycott, then the flood," Mrs. Brown went on. "Mr. Dixon's lost a lot of money. And he's so much in debt, owing so much money on so much property . . . ."

So that was it, thought Amelia. Mr. Dixon wouldn't let them live in the house for free anymore. He wanted them to pay rent. To pay the rent on a house as nice as this one, they'd probably have to cut back quite a lot on expenses.

Amelia thought about it. Being bound out as she was, they didn't pay her anything, but still it must cost a lot of money taking care of her. They gave her new clothes, good food, and even some pocket money. So they couldn't afford it anymore but they didn't want to tell her. Of course, that was it! They were afraid she'd get upset. They didn't know how she'd take it.

"It's all right," she said reassuringly. "I know you've been good to me, with clothes and food and things, but I don't really need it. If you want to cut back, that's all right with me. I don't need much to be happy."

Mrs. Brown looked at her fondly.

"You poor girl," Mrs. Brown said, sadness making her voice slow and heavy. "It's very sweet of you to offer, but I'm afraid it's much worse than that."

Mrs. Brown looked away and sighed

She looked down at her lap and spoke so softly that Amelia could barely hear her.

"The fact is, the store is closing. Mr. Dixon has bought too much property, not only here, but other places too—in Orange, in Culpepper, in Albemarle County. He's so deeply in debt that he can't manage any more. He's decided to close down the store and sell it. We'll have to be moving on, Mr. Brown and I. We won't be able to keep you with us."

Amelia stared at her in shock.

"Not stay with you? But where else can I go? How can I—"

Then it all came back to her—the Court, the Justices, that awful day so long ago. She hardly dared ask the question.

"You don't mean you're sending me back to Williamsburg?"

Mrs. Brown sighed a very deep sigh. She looked like she was on the point of crying also.

"Poor Amelia, I'm so sorry but we don't have any choice. We have to take you back to Williamsburg and let the Court decide what to do with you."

Williamsburg! Amelia stood there like a statue, speechless and immobile. She knew she'd been to Williamsburg once, long ago, but Fredericksburg was all she really knew and remembered. And now she'd have to leave it all—Fredericksburg, the Browns, Doctor Mercer, the apothecary, and Jacob.

Mrs. Brown came over and hugged her. It was something she'd never done before. Then Mrs. Brown stroked her hair while Amelia cried into her apron. Mrs. Brown kept saying that things would turn out all right, but Amelia couldn't believe her. She had an awful feeling that things would never be as good again. The best part of her life would soon be over.

chapter 7

The Browns had waited until the very last minute to tell Amelia what was going to happen. It seemed like she was on her way to Williamsburg practically the next day. She hardly had time to say goodbye to people.

Saying goodbye to Doctor Mercer was hard. With a heavy heart, she returned the book he'd lent her.

"I have to be going away," she explained. "I'm going back to Williamsburg."

She didn't have to say anything more. Everyone but her, it seemed, had known about Mr. Dixon's financial troubles. She was the last to know.

"I'm very sorry to see you go," he said. "I hope you can continue your studies. Do you want to wait for Jacob? He's off on an errand but he should be back very soon. Then you can say goodbye to him also."

Surprisingly, saying goodbye to Jacob was the hardest thing. She thought of the dirty, scruffy boy she'd first seen not so long ago, coming up to her proudly to return the things stolen from her pocket. Now he was a likely, up-and-coming lad, a true apothecary apprentice. Tears came again to her eyes and his eyes were misting too, though he put on a brave face and tried to hide it.

And then she was off to Williamsburg.

It was a long journey, three nights and four days traveling the post road, the one they called the King's Highway. She rode in the back of a wagon and they stopped at inns along the way.

They couldn't afford a private room and she didn't like sharing a bed with people they didn't know, so often they just parked at the inn and slept overnight in the wagon. That way they could take care of the horses and maybe warm themselves up with some food by the fire.

It was late in the afternoon when the carriage finally made it to town and Amelia first got a glimpse of Williamsburg. They drove right through the middle of town down Duke of Gloucester Street.

As they drove along, she forgot for a moment her sadness at leaving Fredericksburg and her fears about the future. She was too busy looking around. Williamsburg seemed so much nicer than she'd imagined. The houses and stores all were large and well-kept up, with walkways and fences and gardens. The streets were full of well-dressed people with fine-looking horses and carriages.

Fredericksburg was a busy town, busier than Williamsburg, but Williamsburg was much grander and more important. Fredericksburg was just a commercial town, a place for loading and unloading ships that came up the Rappahannock River. It was full of stores, warehouses, and sailors.

Williamsburg was the capital of Virginia. It had the House of Burgesses, where the representatives met from all the different counties to make the laws. They had a fine building, finer than she'd ever seen before, but the house where the Governor lived was even more magnificent.

The Governor Lord Dunmore, Mr. Brown explained, was the most important person in Virginia. Even the House of Burgesses had to report to him and he had power over them. The Governor was appointed by King George himself.

The Governor's house was called the Governor's Palace, said Mr. Brown. It really was a palace, thought Amelia, like something fit for a King and Queen.

It lay far back from the road with a great park in front of it, stretching all the way from the palace walls to Duke of Gloucester Street. Behind the red brick wall, guarded by a lion and a unicorn of stone, there was a great complex of buildings and gardens. The main building was three stories tall and topped by two great chimneys and a fine white cupola, with two large buildings in front on either side and any number of other buildings behind it, including the stables, carriage house, kitchen, scullery, laundry, and dairy, buildings for salting and smoking meats and for storing ice, wine, coal, and charcoal. There were the usual "necessaries" or privies of course, but in addition there was even a special octagonal building just for bathing!

Amelia's journey ended at the Bruton Parish Church. Mr. Brown patted her cheek and sadly said good-bye, and then he handed her over to the Reverend Henley. He would look after her, Mr. Brown said, until the vestrymen and the Court decided what to do with her.

Reverend Henley was a kindly man. Amelia very much hoped she could stay and work for him. Unfortunately for her, it was not to be. All too soon, the decision was made. She was given to the bricklayer, Mr. Pryor.

chapter 8

Working for Mr. and Mrs. Pryor wasn't anything like working for the Browns but at first it wasn't unbearable. Amelia had Miss Clarke to thank for that, not that she thanked her at the time. In fact, Amelia thought Miss Clarke was pretty mean to her. It was only later on, when Miss Clarke was gone, that Amelia realized that Mr. Pryor was ever so much worse.

Miss Clarke was Mrs. Pryor's sister. She'd come to Williamsburg from Surry, Virginia, just across the James River from Williamsburg.

For some time now, Mrs. Pryor had been quite ill, so Miss Clarke came to help her. Mrs. Pryor was on the mend, but she was still too weak to do much of anything. Mrs. Pryor spent most of the day in bed and Miss Clarke was the one who ran the household.

Miss Clarke seemed very old to Amelia. She wasn't quite as ancient as Amelia thought she was, but she was well along in her forties. She'd never married, maybe because she had a pockmarked face, a squinty eye, and a grouchy and snappish disposition.

Miss Clarke was strict but she was also fair. So long as Amelia kept up with her chores and minded her manners, Miss Clarke left her pretty much alone and didn't punish her.

Keeping up with her chores, though, wasn't so easy to do. From the time she rose before dawn until late at night, Amelia was constantly working. Not only did she help in the kitchen like she'd done for the Browns, but she did just about everything else that you could imagine. She ran errands, swept and cleaned, lit and tended the fires, weeded the garden, and helped with the laundry.

She also helped take care of the stable. This was the part she liked the very best. Mr. Pryor had four very sweet and handsome horses. Mr. Pryor had someone to take care of them, of course—John Wilton was the groom and driver. John had a very high opinion of himself and he only did the things he thought were important. Amelia was happy to spend time in the stable doing whatever he didn't do and he was happy to let her.

Sometimes it was just impossible to do all her chores and then Miss Clarke would take a stick to her. Miss Clarke wasn't angry and she didn't hit Amelia terribly hard, but she wouldn't listen to any excuses. She thought that if she punished Amelia every time anything didn't get done, then the next time Amelia would try harder to finish her chores.

Amelia had a bit of a temper and sometimes she was quick to speak her mind, so "minding her manners" was even more of a problem than getting her chores done. Miss Clarke would get very angry if Amelia said something she didn't like or she thought Amelia was being sassy.

Then she'd tell Mr. Pryor and he'd be the one to punish her. When Mr. Pryor used the switch, he swung it a good deal harder.

One time, John left the stable door open and one of the horses got into the garden. The horse ate the turnips right out of the ground, so many and so fast that he might have even died, if he hadn't been stopped in time.

It was John's fault, no question about that, but he blamed it on Amelia and Miss Clarke believed him. Amelia tried to protest but Miss Clarke wouldn't even listen. It was so unfair! And John just stood there smirking and laughing to himself, like he thought it was funny. That was just too much!

Amelia got so upset that she lost her temper. She said John was nothing but a nasty, awful liar and Miss Clarke was a horrible, stupid old woman for believing him.

Of course then Miss Clarke got very angry, thinking now Amelia had done three things wrong—leaving the door open, lying about it, and then saying such awful, rude and insulting things on top of it all. The first punishment wasn't enough, Miss Clarke declared angrily, as Amelia clearly hadn't learned her lesson. So she told Mr. Pryor he needed to punish her too.

Mr. Pryor got so mad that he locked her in the smokehouse. The smokehouse wasn't a nice sort of place, just a square little building without any windows. It was called

It wasn't a nice sort of place

a smokehouse because that's where they smoked the hams and fish and meats that needed to be preserved from spoiling. Inside, it had hooks hanging all around the top and a place made of bricks in the center of the floor where you could build a fire.

The hams and bacons would be salted first and then hung on the hooks. Then they'd make a very smoky fire and let the meats hang there for a long time with the smoke all around them. The smoke would flavor the meats and help keep them longer from spoiling.

Amelia was left in the smokehouse overnight. There wasn't a fire, which was good because the smoke might have killed her. Without a fire, though, it was very cold and dark. As tired as she was, she could hardly sleep for shivering.

As she lay there on the dirt floor, she couldn't help but feel totally miserable. She thought of Mr. and Mrs. Brown, and Doctor Mercer, and Jacob. How were they doing now? How she wished that she could see them again!

Her last thought, before she fell asleep at last, was to hope that they were better off than she was.

chapter 9

After Amelia had been in Williamsburg a couple of weeks, things sort of settled down as much as they were going to. She figured out the best way to do her chores so she could finish them faster. That made things a lot smoother. She didn't always do them as well as before but Miss Clarke didn't seem to notice that.

Amelia tried to stay out of trouble and mostly she did. Sometimes, though she was so tired and unhappy that she'd get upset and forget to do something important. Or she'd say something that made Miss Clarke mad and get into extra-big trouble. She kept thinking that it was all so unfair, but she knew there was no use complaining. She pretty quickly learned it was best if she could avoid Mr. Pryor and Miss Clarke altogether.

It wouldn't have been so bad, she told herself, if she hadn't had to give up her studying.

To begin with, she had hardly a moment of free time. She was busy from before the sun came up until well into the dark of the night time. Even if she could have found the time, she didn't have anything to study. There wasn't anyone to lend her books and Mr. Pryor didn't have a library to speak of. She still dreamed of being a doctor or apothecary but, as time went on, she could feel her dream was fading away.

The pity of it was, she was reminded of it over and over again. There seemed to be apothecaries everywhere she went in Williamsburg.

For a while, Doctor Carter's was her favorite. He had the most wonderful shop sign—"The Unicorn's Horn." She even went inside two times, once to pick up some Essential Salt of Lemon to take stains out of linen clothes, and another time for some of Doctor Norris's Drops when Miss Josephine the cook had a fever.

Doctor Carter sold many more different kinds of things than Doctor Mercer had. He had medicines and medical equipment of course, just like Doctor Mercer only more so. He carried fancy imported goods and spices, like mustard, anchovies, and oil, ginger, nutmeg, and cinnamon, sweet-smelling lavender and flower waters, and fancy sweetmeats like rock sugar candy and sugared almonds. He also had all sorts of patent medicines imported from London, with impressive names like Turlington's Balsam of Life and Royal Imperial Golden Stuff, as well as the Daffy's Elixir that Miss Elizabeth in Fredericksburg had liked so much.

Amelia would have been happy to go see Doctor Carter over and over again, especially since one time he'd given her a bit of barley sugar. Doctor Galt was the one treating Mrs. Pryor, however, and Miss Clarke was the one who always went to see him.

After a while, Amelia decided that Doctor Galt was better even than Doctor Carter. For one thing, he was a very educated man. He'd even studied in London. Every time she went by his shop (which she often did, since his shop was right there on Duke of Gloucester Street), she'd linger as long as she dared, standing there on tippy-toe and looking in the window.

She imagined Doctor Galt must have lots of books, since he'd studied in London. How she wished she could ask him to lend her books and teach her! Of course she couldn't do it, though. She was just a servant and a total stranger. He'd think she was the rudest, most impertinent girl. He might even think she was crazy.

His shop was right there on
Duke of Gloucester Street

The brightest spot in Amelia's day, besides spending time with the horses, was helping Miss Josephine in the kitchen. She was a large and imposing woman and a very fine cook, and she wasn't afraid of anybody. Even Mr. Pryor, as mean as he was, was careful not to make her too angry.

Miss Josephine was enslaved because her parents were slaves, but she was born right there in Williamsburg. The Warrens, the people she'd worked for before, had taught her to read and write so she could cook them good things from recipes. Like Mr. Dixon, though, they'd gotten too far into debt and then, to pay it off, they'd had to sell her to Mr. Pryor.

Amelia didn't understand how anyone could own another human being and buy and sell them, just like a pig or a piece of furniture. She'd tried asking about it at first but after a while she gave up, as no one had ever been able to explain it to her.

Like Miss Elizabeth before, Miss Josephine seemed to like Amelia. It was a good thing too. Sometimes, when Miss Clarke wasn't happy with what Amelia had done, she'd make her work straight through her supper. Amelia would have been pretty hungry then if Miss Josephine hadn't saved some food for her.

The most wonderful thing about Miss Josephine, however, was that she knew so much about medicine. Amelia didn't realize how much she knew for the longest time, not until one day when she had a terrible headache. It hurt so much that she could hardly stand it. She was very much afraid that she'd do a bad job of her chores and Miss Clarke would end up punishing her.

"Here, drink this," Josephine told her that morning, when Amelia had told her about the headache. She shoved a mug of liquid in Amelia's hand. It smelled pretty horrid.

"Don't mind how it smells," said Miss Josephine, "just drink it down. After a little while, you'll feel a lot better. In the meantime, you can sit over there and pretend you're keeping an eye on the biscuits." And she pointed to a stool by the fireplace.

Amelia obediently drank the liquid down. Luckily it didn't taste as bad as it smelled, so she held her nose and drank it quickly. After fifteen minutes or so, to Amelia's great surprise, her headache vanished entirely.

Maybe she shouldn't have been so surprised, Amelia realized afterwards. Now that she thought of it, the cook had her own sort of medical practice. People—other enslaved people, but other kinds of people too—would sometimes show up at the kitchen door with some sort of injury or illness. Miss Josephine had been treating people all along, only Amelia had never really noticed.

"What was in that drink?" she asked. "It's like it was magic. Are you a doctor too? Did the Warrens teach you medicine?"

Miss Josephine laughed at that.

"It's no magic, honey," she said, chuckling, "and I didn't need the Warrens to teach me. My mother taught me, that's what it was. Now get back to your chores before Miss Clarke comes along and sees you wasting your time here in the kitchen."

So Amelia got up and went back to work. After that, she started spending as much time as she could in the kitchen and Miss Josephine would teach her. Snakeroot, ginseng, chickweed, plantain, purslaine, marsh-mallow, rosemary, nettles—any sort of plant that grew in Virginia, Miss Josephine seemed to know all about it. She knew how to grow it or where it grew, whether you used the roots or the leaves or the flowers or what, and what sort of ailments it was good for. She didn't know about man-made things like Doctor Norris's Drops and Royal Imperial Golden Stuff and other fancy patent medicines, but when it came to herbs and plants, she was almost as good as *Domestic Medicine.*

Amelia began to feel that, the way things were, her life was almost bearable. Unfortunately, all too soon Miss Clarke went back to Surry and Mr. Pryor took over running the household.

chapter 10

Miss Clarke left suddenly one day, without any warning.

"I have to leave now," she told Mr. Pryor that morning. "My father is ailing and I'm needed in Surry. Mrs. Pryor is coming along well enough. Someone else can take care of her."

Mr. Pryor tried to argue, but her mind was made up. She gathered up her things and Mr. Pryor took her to the ferry.

Right away, almost the instant Miss Clarke was gone, Amelia's life got very much harder.

Miss Clarke was hard but she was fair, for the most part. Mr. Pryor was very much harder and he wasn't fair at all. Sometimes it seemed like he'd punish you for nothing. Some days, he was in such a bad mood that you could hardly escape being punished for something, whether you did anything or not.

Even so, it wasn't the punishments that made life so hard. The worst thing was that the mood in the house was so depressing. The Pryor's house was never a very cheery place, but at least when Miss Clarke was there, it was peaceful and things ran pretty smoothly. With Mr. Pryor in charge, however, no one ever knew what was coming next, but they knew it would always be something awful.

Amelia did her best to keep up her spirits. More and more, though, she felt a sense of hopelessness creeping over her. Being a doctor began to seem like only a beautiful dream. The reality was so very different. It seemed that she'd be living like this forever. There was nothing to look forward to and no sign that things might ever change.

The one bright spot in Amelia's daily life (apart from the horses) was Miss Josephine. Miss Josephine was still teaching her about roots and flowers and herbs. The problem was, there was hardly any time for it. Mr. Pryor had a habit of checking in on his servants at odd times to make sure they were always hard at work and never resting or taking it easy.

Miss Josephine didn't have to worry about this so much. She could always say she was watching over the fire or keeping an eye on how things were cooking. Heaven help

Amelia, though, if Mr. Pryor found her just sitting in the kitchen, listening to Miss Josephine!

Another problem was that a lot of people didn't respect Miss Josephine's kind of learning. No matter how much Amelia knew, unless she could say she'd studied with a doctor or apothecary, a lot of people wouldn't trust her to take care of them.

Just when she was about to give up, however, a miracle occurred. Well, it wasn't a miracle in ordinary terms—not walking on water or anything like that. To Amelia, however, it was just as good as. One day, Mr. Pryor sent her to Doctor Galt's shop to pick up Mrs. Pryor's medicine.

After so long just trying to look in the window as she passed by, even walking through the door into the shop was thrilling. Once she was inside, she just stood there looking around. She stood there so long that Doctor Galt began to look at her with considerable suspicion.

"You there," he said at last, rather sharply. "Yes, you! What is your business here?"

Amelia looked up at him in surprise. She'd been so interested in reading all the labels on all the different jars that she'd almost forgotten about everything else, including why she came there.

"Please Sir," she said as politely as she could, "I'm come to get Mrs. Pryor's medicine."

He looked at her doubtfully.

She just stood there looking around

"Who are you? I haven't seen you before. What happened to Miss Clarke and Mr. Pryor?"

"Miss Clarke has gone home and Mr. Pryor's too busy, so he sent me. I'm Amelia. I work for Mr. Pryor."

Doctor Galt studied her for a long, long time, and all the while he was frowning.

"He doesn't believe me!" Amelia thought. She was starting to feel a sense of panic. Was he going to send her away? What would Mr. Pryor do to her if she came back without the medicine?

"So you're Amelia," he said coldly. "You've certainly taken your time, my girl. I expected you long before this."

"Expected me?" Amelia's eyes were wide. Of all the things she'd been afraid he might say, this was the very last thing entirely.

"Doctor Mercer wrote to me about you," he went on, still frowning. "He said you were interested in learning more about medicine. I told him I'd be happy to help. I even picked out some books from my library. I was all prepared but you never came, so I figured you weren't really interested. I wasn't entirely surprised. Just a passing fancy, was it?"

It took her several seconds to understand what he was saying, it was so unexpected. Then the words came out in a rush, anxious and earnest and pleading.

"Oh no! I mean, yes, I am. Oh so terribly! Interested, I mean. I never—I didn't think—" she broke off, realizing she was making very little sense. "Oh would you? Help me learn, I mean? Would you really?"

"So why didn't you come to see me long before this? I suppose you'll tell me you were too busy? You young people these days, you're flighty as butterflies, and young girls especially. I was ready to help you then but I don't know about it now. Why should I waste my time on you?"

"Please, Doctor Galt," she begged, hoping he'd understand and believe her. "I would have come right away, but how would I have known that I could come here? How would I know that you were willing to teach me?"

"Doctor Mercer wrote to you, that's how. Didn't you get his letter?"

Amelia's face showed her surprise.

"A letter from Doctor Mercer? No, I never did. He wrote to me? Did he really?"

"Hmm, no letter. Is that it?" He studied her for a moment, considering. She looked and sounded so surprised and confused that he decided to believe her. "These letters do get lost, I suppose. I suppose that could explain it. My own cousin says he wrote me a letter several months ago, but it never arrived."

He shrugged his shoulders as if to say "some things can't be helped" and he looked at her sympathetically.

"Well anyway, here you are now. Would you like to borrow one of my books? Doctor Mercer said you were studying *Domestic Medicine*. I must say, I'm surprised. That's a pretty serious book. How far had you gotten in reading it?"

Amelia suddenly felt ever so much better. He wasn't mad at her! He would teach her!

"I've been studying about the different kinds of fevers so far," she said eagerly, "though sometimes Doctor Mercer taught me from other sections. I had almost finished the parts on fevers when I had to leave Fredericksburg."

"All right then. Doctor Mercer must think quite a lot of you. He sent me the money to buy you your very own copy of *Domestic Medicine*. I ordered it when I got his letter, but it may be quite a while before it gets here. You can borrow my own copy in the meantime."

Amelia was stunned. Doctor Mercer had given him money to buy her a book of her very own?

"Thank you, Doctor Mercer," she murmured softly to herself. "Thank you, thank you, thank you!"

Doctor Galt disappeared into the back and came out holding the familiar heavy, leather-bound book. Then he laid it on the counter.

"Here it is. I expect you to take good care of it. You can study it for a while on your own and then I'd like to see how much you've learned from it. Come back in a week or so and I'll examine you."

Amelia left the shop clutching the book under her arm. She was in such a happy daze that she forgot all about Mrs. Pryor's medicine. Luckily she remembered before she'd gone very far and she ran back to get it.

As she made her way back to Mr. Pryor's house, she couldn't help feeling sorry that she hadn't known to go see Doctor Galt much sooner. Of course, she couldn't have known that he was waiting for her to come by, but so many days had been wasted.

Letters get lost, Doctor Galt had said, but she didn't think that was the reason. She could understand a letter getting lost if it came from far away, like London or France, or even Vermont or Massachusetts. It wasn't so far to Williamsburg from Fredericksburg, however. The post road was straight and direct. She knew this first-hand, as she'd traveled it herself when Mr. Brown brought her to Williamsburg. So there wasn't really much chance for a letter to go astray.

Amelia was sure that Doctor Mercer's letter to her had really arrived, only Mr. Pryor hadn't given it to her. Of all the things he'd done so far, she thought, this was surely the very worst of them.

chapter 11

When Amelia got back to Mr. Pryor's, she hid the book carefully in the loft of the stable. She was totally certain that she couldn't let Mr. Pryor know what she was doing.

That was yet another thing that didn't seem right to her. He should be encouraging her to learn things, not punishing her. After all, wasn't he supposed to be teaching her things so she could be on her own one day, when she was older? That's how Mrs. Brown had explained it. The orphans were given to other people to raise, since they didn't have parents who could do it. They were more like apprentices than just servants.

Of course she had to work to earn her keep, but Mr. Pryor was supposed to teach her something useful so that someday she could make a living on her own. The way he treated her, though, you'd think he owned her outright, body and soul, just like he owned Miss Josephine or poor Penney.

Thinking of Penney, Amelia always felt sad. Penney was about her age, with creamy brown skin and a pert, pretty face. She was kind and smart and she never had a bad word for anyone. She worked wherever she was told—in the garden, in the kitchen, even in the brick yard. As badly as Mr. Pryor treated Amelia, he treated Penney even worse. Amelia felt so sorry for her, she tried to do something nice for Penney whenever she could.

Amelia was afraid Mr. Pryor would find out about Doctor Galt and the book, but that wasn't going to stop her. She studied late into the night whenever she could manage it, by the light of the moon when it was full enough, and by the fire or stubs of candles when it wasn't. Often in the morning she felt like she'd hardly slept at all and her eyes were strained and blurry. But she kept on.

The first time she went back to see Doctor Galt, he questioned her very thoroughly. When he was done, she looked at him anxiously. Had she done well enough? It seemed to her that she must have forgotten a lot of things since she left Fredericksburg.

"All right then, keep on," was all he said, but he seemed to be satisfied.

Amelia left feeling proud and happy. She hadn't felt this happy since she came to Williamsburg.

The next time she went in to pick up something from Doctor Galt, he had a big surprise for her.

"Here, this came for you," he said, handing her a letter.

"A letter for me?"

She took the little packet of folded paper and carefully examined it. It was closed with a bright red wax seal and addressed in nice, legible handwriting.

"To Amelia," it said "care of Doctor Galt, Duke of Gloucester Street, Williamsburg, Virginia." The sender's name and address were written there also.

"It's from Doctor Mercer!" she said happily. Then she looked at the address again curiously. Why did he write her care of Doctor Galt? Did Doctor Mercer tell him she'd never gotten the letter before? Did he also suspect that Mr. Pryor never gave it to her?

"I told him how you were coming along." Doctor Galt said it blandly, like he didn't have anything particular in mind, but his next words answered her unspoken question. "I suggested that he send a letter here if he wanted to write to you. This letter arrived practically right away. Go ahead, you can open it and read it."

So she opened it excitedly.

It was full of news and encouragement. He was glad to hear of her from Doctor Galt, Doctor Mercer wrote.

Doctor Galt had told him that she was making good progress and she should keep on studying hard. Mr. and Mrs. Brown were both well. They were still in Fredericksburg but soon they'd be moving far to the west, to Winchester. Jacob was doing just fine and sent his very best regards to her.

It was all good news, and the very best news was at the end. Sometime later on, the letter said, Doctor Mercer might even send Jacob on an errand to Williamsburg. How wonderful it would be to see him!

"A good letter, then?" Doctor Galt asked, seeing how pleased she was.

"Wonderful." She carefully folded up the letter and put it in her pocket, turning her face away from Doctor Galt in order to hide her tears. It was so wonderful to hear from everyone in Fredericksburg, to know they were all well and thinking of her. At the same time, however, it reminded her that they were so far away. She missed them all so terribly.

chapter 12

After that, things went on fairly calmly for a while, without anything very wonderful or very terrible happening. Amelia might almost have said things weren't so bad if it hadn't been for Christmas.

Maybe she wouldn't have minded so much if Christmas hadn't been so special when she was in Fredericksburg. Mr. and Mrs. Brown celebrated the full twelve days, from the night before Christmas until the sixth day of the New Year, the day when the Three Kings had arrived with gifts for the little baby Jesus.

In Fredericksburg with the Browns, the house was decorated top to bottom with greenery. Just about every shelf, pitcher, pot, fireplace mantel, or windowsill in the house was filled with cuttings or festooned with garlands of evergreens. There was pine, rosemary, holly, ivy, and laurel—whatever they could find in the way of greenery. There were even little sprigs of holly with red berries stuck to every window pane and bunches of mistletoe hanging from the ceiling.

The house smelled wonderful with all the evergreens and with all the cooking and baking. During Christmastime, everyone in Fredericksburg would go visiting family and friends. So the Browns made sure to have special things to give their guests to eat and drink, like cakes and punch and syllabub. It was all so delicious and so much fun that Amelia didn't even mind the extra work with all the cooking.

Amelia remembered the last Christmas especially well. To her it was the best Christmas ever. The Browns had a party on Twelfth Night and let her come to it, not as a servant, but as one of the guests. She'd almost never had so much fun as that evening.

Someone had brought a flute and someone else had brought a fiddle. They played music and people danced, and then they played songs and hymns that people could sing to. "Joy to the World" was her favorite.

Then people played games. One of the women playing the card game of whist let Amelia look over her shoulder. "You bring me luck," the woman said, and maybe it was true because she kept on winning. The players were betting a few pence on every game and the woman even gave Amelia some of the money she won.

There were lots of good things to eat as well, candied fruit and other sweetmeats, jellies with whipped cream, baked apples with icing, and little cakes studded with almonds.

It was well after midnight when everyone left and Amelia finally went to sleep. In her dreams, she kept on dancing.

This year, Amelia didn't have any great expectations. She knew that Christmas at Mr. Pryor's would never be as wonderful as it had been in Fredericksburg. She'd dared to hope, though, that it might be a little bit special in some way or another. Everyone had to be a little bit nicer at Christmas, she thought. Even Mr. Pryor.

How wrong she was.

As Christmastime came nearer and nearer, Amelia began to wonder. There was nothing different going on at all. No baking, no decorations, no greenery. No preparations for visitors at all.

"Don't go thinking Christmas is an excuse to get lazy," Mr. Pryor told all the servants, right before Christmas

There were lots of good things to eat

started. "I don't want any Christmas foolishness, do you hear me? If I catch you taking time away from your duties for anything—anything at all—you'll get a beating."

Then he looked straight at Amelia, his expression as mean as anything. "That especially means you, you worthless little girl. So you'd better not try to get away with anything."

There weren't any candles in Mr. Pryor's windows, not a single one. No candles, no music, and no laughter. Even Christmas Day would have been just an ordinary day, except that Miss Josephine insisted on going to Bruton

Parish Church for the Christmas service and she took Amelia with her.

At first Mr. Pryor refused to let them go, but Miss Josephine stood up to him.

"If you won't let me go to church on Christmas day," she told him, "I'll go tell Reverend Henley."

Mr. Pryor hardly ever cared about anyone's opinion, but he must have cared about Reverend Henley's at least a little. He looked very annoyed but he finally gave in and let them go.

Amelia thought the church looked very fine with its high box pews, tall windows, and the towering wooden pulpit. Everything was decorated with greenery and it smelled like rosemary and pine trees. The best thing, though, was the music.

Most of the year, there was only one thing you could sing in church and that was the psalms of David. You could have organ music though and the organist was very fine. The sound of the organ filled the church and made up for the lack of singing. The music was so resonant and loud that Amelia could even feel it.

Since it was Christmas, though, there was one special hymn they could sing, that you could only sing at Christmas. It was "While Shepherds Watched Their Fields by Night." Everyone knew all the words and sang it most enthusiastically. The singing was so loud that you could hardly even hear the organ.

When the service was over, Christmas was over too, at least for Amelia.

The rest of Christmas day, Mr. Pryor was in an even worse mood than usual, if that was possible. He made sure that everyone else in the house was even more miserable than he was.

He paid special attention to Amelia, it seemed, like he wanted her to be the most miserable one in the household. All that day, he kept giving her more and more things to do. He'd criticize everything she did and make her do it over and over again. Right before he went to bed, he gave her even more chores and said they'd better be done by the morning. By the time she finished everything she had to do, it was after midnight.

When she finally lay down to sleep, Amelia couldn't help but cry. It was the saddest Christmas day ever in her life.

chapter 13

After Christmas Day, there were still eleven more days of Christmastime. Everywhere else in Williamsburg, the festive times were still going on. When Amelia walked down the street, she could hear music and people singing and laughing. It was just like Fredericksburg, she thought. Maybe even better.

Amelia didn't laugh with the others, though, and she didn't linger around to look at the decorations or listen to the singing. After Mr. Pryor's warning, she was extra careful what she did and didn't do.

Mr. Pryor had been right to warn them, because the least little thing could lead to punishment. He punished the groom and driver John for visiting his sister in town and coming home quite merry. One of the maids was punished for lingering too long on her errands, as she stopped to talk with friends or to wish people Merry Christmas. Then John was punished again for singing a hymn while he brushed down the horses. Miss Josephine was especially mad about that.

"Can't even sing a hymn," she grumbled, "and here it is Christmas. It isn't Christian of him, is what I say." But she didn't say anything like that to Mr. Pryor. She only muttered it to herself in the kitchen.

It was bad enough, thought Amelia, to be so miserable at Christmastime, without being punished extra hard. She felt like she was walking on eggshells all the time, trying not to crush a single one of them. If she did get punished for something that wasn't fair, she was pretty sure she'd get mad and say something back to Mr. Pryor. Of course, that would make things even worse. She didn't want to end up freezing cold and hungry in the smokehouse.

It was only on the very last night, on the twelfth night when Christmastime would end, that Amelia took a chance of getting into terrible trouble. That night the Governor had a ball at the Governor's Palace and she sneaked out late at night just to see it.

The sky was so clear that it seemed like she could see every single one of the stars. There were so many that the sky was almost white in places. There were great tall torches burning all around the outside of the

Governor's Palace to light the way, and candles in every single window. Many of the other houses and even shops had candles in their windows too, flickering and glowing in the darkness.

It was so cold that Amelia shivered in her thin wool cape and her toes and fingers grew numb, but it was worth it. Between the host of stars above and the torch and candle lights below, the night seemed truly magical. It was as if some of the stars had come down from the sky in order to light the town.

All the time, though, she felt anxious and afraid. What if Mr. Pryor caught her? She gave a great sigh of relief when she closed the kitchen door behind her. She'd made it back safely!

Even the next day though, Amelia was still worried that she might have been discovered. When Mr. Pryor sent for her to come up to Mrs. Pryor's room, she was sure that he'd somehow found out what she'd done.

When she got up to Mrs. Pryor's room she hardly dared go into it. It turned out to be Mrs. Pryor, though, who wanted to see her. Mrs. Pryor had felt worse than usual, apparently, and she'd used up all her pills. She told Amelia to go to the apothecary right away and get her more medicine.

Mr. Pryor was there in her room at the time, so he heard Mrs. Pryor say it. So there wasn't any doubt that's what Amelia was supposed to do. Even so, when Amelia left the house, she felt nervous.

She'd only just walked into the apothecary, barely through the door, when someone came up behind and put his hands over her eyes like a blindfold. It happened so suddenly that she didn't even have time to feel afraid. Then she heard a familiar voice.

"Surprise! Can you guess who it is?"

"Jacob! Is it really you?" she exclaimed joyfully. "What are you doing here?"

"Doctor Mercer sent me. He's run out of Peruvian bark and he wanted me to see if I could buy or borrow any here in Williamsburg."

"How is he? How are you? How are the Browns? What is the news in Fredericksburg?"

Her words all came out in a rush, without even a pause for breathing.

"So many questions!" Jacob smiled. "Well, I'll try to answer them. Doctor Mercer is fine. I'm fine. The Browns left Fredericksburg just before Christmas. They were sorry to miss all the parties and such, but they were afraid the weather would get too bad if they waited. That's all the news in a nutshell."

"That's it?" Amelia made a face, pretending to be mad at him. "That's only the littlest bit of news, almost nothing at all. You must tell me every single detail!"

So he did, and time went by quickly. Suddenly she realized how late it was.

"Oh, dear!" Amelia cried.

Jacob looked at Amelia with concern.

"What's the matter?"

"I've forgotten the time. Now I'll surely get a beating."

Doctor Galt looked down at her over the rims of
his glasses.

"Surely not a beating for such a little thing?"

"Mr. Pryor's very strict," Amelia said miserably, "and
lately he's been even worse than usual."

"Hmm." Doctor Galt looked thoughtful for a moment.
Then it seemed that he had an inspiration.

"I'll tell you what. You can tell Mr. Pryor that the pills
weren't made up when you got here and I told you to wait
for them. You can tell him to ask me himself if he doesn't
believe you."

In fact, the pills were already made up. They were there
in a little pile, in front of Doctor Galt on the counter. He
took half of them away and put them back in a jar. Then
he wrapped the rest in a piece of paper, tied it up tight,
and handed it to Amelia.

"You can say that I was so busy and it took so long to make up the pills that you only got half of them. Say that I told you to come back for the rest of them tomorrow. Come by in the morning, fairly early on. That way you can see Jacob again before he goes back to Fredericksburg."

chapter 14

Once Christmastime was over and done with, things went pretty much back to normal. For most of January, to Amelia's great relief, Mr. Pryor hardly paid her any attention. He was too busy with his lawsuit.

Penney had finally had enough, it seemed, and it wasn't just missing all the joy of Christmas. No one was talking about it, but Amelia could tell that something really terrible had happened. Penney had run away but she hadn't gone very far, just to a plantation not far outside of Williamsburg. The Lambertsons—that was the name of the people who owned the plantation—they had taken her in and refused to give her back again.

Mr. Pryor was in a rage. He had his lawyer over and insisted on suing Mr. Lambertson. Amelia could hear him shouting all the way down the hall. Since his office was in the front of the building facing the street, probably everyone passing by the house could hear him.

She's mine, she belongs to me," Mr. Pryor stormed. "Mr. Lambertson's a thief, a criminal! How dare he steal her away from me! I want her back and I want him arrested too."

"Now, now, Mr. Pryor," the lawyer began, trying to talk calmly, but Mr. Pryor cut him off in mid-sentence.

"Don't now, now me," he yelled. "You're my lawyer and I'm paying you. So do what I say. I'm right and you know it."

"I'm your lawyer and I know the law," the lawyer responded, clearly angry himself but more dignified, "and you don't. That's why you're paying me. It's not as simple as you seem to think. If you listen to me, however, and if it's true what you say, then I can get Penney back for you."

After that, they both lowered their voices, so Amelia never learned the rest of it. All she knew was that Mr. Pryor had it constantly on his mind, so he wasn't paying so much attention to other things.

Amelia was grateful that Mr. Pryor was leaving her alone, though she was sorry for the reason why. Every night, she said a little prayer that Penney could stay with the Lambertsons.

Finally the court day came and Amelia crossed her fingers for the outcome. When Mr. Pryor came home all smiling, she felt sad. He must have won the lawsuit, to be smiling so. The next day Penney came home as well. She didn't say much and Amelia didn't ask her.

After that, Mr. Pryor went back to his usual self. He was worse than usual, if anything. Amelia would look up from her work and he'd be there. He seemed always to be keeping an eye on her. At least he was better to Penney, or so it seemed. Amelia had the idea that Miss Josephine was responsible for that. She must have said something to him and she must have been pretty mad. Mr. Pryor seemed even more afraid of her than usual.

Amelia kept on just the same, but she tried to be especially careful. She needed a good excuse to see Doctor Galt, so she didn't see him very often and her visits were always short ones.

She kept on studying but she had to do it at night, when she was supposed to be sleeping. She slept in the kitchen these days, on the floor by the fireplace. The kitchen was a separate little building away from the house, so she thought it was pretty private. She'd read there at night by the light of the fire, until the fire was too low and her eyes were too blurry.

The trouble was, she didn't get much time for sleeping. With all the work she had to do, she was busy from early morning until late at night. Then she'd have to stay up even later still if she wanted to study *Domestic Medicine*.

She slept on the floor by the fireplace

Often she missed so much sleep that during the day she wandered around only half-awake, easily confused and more than usually clumsy.

Miss Josephine guessed what she was doing but she didn't tell her to stop.

"You'd best take care," was all she said. "You'll be getting yourself in a world of trouble."

Amelia thought she was taking care. She thought she was safe, but she wasn't.

chapter 15

"Aha, I've caught you at last, you ungrateful piece of baggage!"

With these angry words and a blow from Mr. Pryor's walking stick, that was how Amelia was awakened. She had fallen asleep by the fire with *Domestic Medicine* open before her, and he'd caught her.

She tried to scoot out of the way but Mr. Pryor grabbed the book and waved it in her face.

"Domestic Medicine—what is this? Where did you get this from? You little thief, you must have stolen it!"

"No, please, I didn't steal it," Amelia cried, trying to snatch it back from him. He held her off, holding his walking stick up like a club and threatening to strike her with it.

"Two times a thief, that's what you are, and shameless too—you haven't even got the decency to admit it. I knew something was going on and now I've finally caught you at it. You've stolen the book and you're also stealing time from me, the time that I own, that you owe me. This book is going in the fire and I'll whip you within an inch of your life, if I ever find you reading again."

With that, he started toward the fireplace.

"No, please, no!" She tried to get between him and the fire, despite his still holding out the stick like a weapon. "It isn't my book. I borrowed it."

He turned and gave her a stony stare.

"Who lent it to you? I'll fix him too. How dare he, corrupting my servants!"

Almost too late, she realized she couldn't tell him about Doctor Galt. If she did, he'd make sure she never saw him again. He might even try to get Doctor Galt in trouble too. She bit her tongue and kept silent.

"You can't tell me, can you?" Mr. Pryor said with a smug, evil grin. "That's because you stole it. Of course no one lent it to you, a stupid, ignorant girl like you."

Then he threw the book in the fireplace.

The fire had been banked down for the night, but when the book landed amidst the coals, it stirred them up again. The sparks flew and the fire began to come to life.

"No, no!" Heedless of the fire, Amelia reached in to rescue the book before it started burning. She felt a stab of pain as Mr. Pryor whacked at her arm with the stick, but still she reached out for the book, to save it.

Mr. Prior grabbed her roughly and yanked her away from the fire. Then he lifted her up off the floor and shook her angrily.

"You worthless girl," he shouted, "how dare you disobey me! It was an evil day that I ever agreed to take you."

With that, he dragged her out of the room and across the yard and threw her roughly into the smokehouse. Lying there on the dirt floor, she could hear him turn the key in the door, locking her in there, in the darkness.

It was only then that she realized how much her arm was

hurting. It wasn't just the blow from the cane. She must have burned it too, trying to save the book from burning.

Amelia wrapped her apron around her wounded arm and closed her eyes. She tried to ignore the pain and waited for the morning. Her last thought before she finally fell asleep was what she would tell Doctor Galt. She'd lost his precious book, his *Domestic Medicine*. He'd be so angry!

He'd never teach her anything again, Amelia thought miserably. After what had happened to his book, he'd never lend her another one. Her dream of being a doctor was over.

chapter 16

Amelia was so tired that she slept a long time despite the pain in her arm, lying there on the floor in the darkness. It was well after dawn when she finally woke up. She could tell by a tiny crack of light that showed at one edge of the door, where it didn't fit quite tightly enough.

"Why didn't they wake me up?" she wondered, thinking of all the work she had to do. Sweeping out and lighting the fires, giving Mr. and Mrs. Pryor their coffee, washing up after breakfast, making up the beds, cleaning the rooms, feeding and brushing the horses, helping Miss Josephine in the kitchen. When I do get out, she thought to herself, I'll have a hard time all day, trying to catch up with everything.

But no one came to let her out. All day long, she was locked in the smokehouse. She was hungry and thirsty and her arm still hurt, and despite it's being day, it was dark in there.

Finally, at dusk, Miss Josephine came and unlocked the door.

"You poor thing," was all she said. She helped Amelia up, led her slowly back to the kitchen, and sat her down on the stool by the fireplace. Then she gave Amelia a cup full of water and a hunk of cheese and bread.

Amelia was thirsty as could be, but she didn't drink all of the water. She dipped her apron in the water and started to dab at her arm, trying to clean off the dirt and ashes.

"Oh!" When she touched her burn, she couldn't help but cry out in pain.

"What's wrong with your arm?" Miss Josephine said sharply. Then she came over to see for herself what the problem was.

Miss Josephine saw the burn right away and also some ugly bruises that Amelia hadn't even noticed before. That must be where Mr. Pryor had grabbed her, Amelia realized.

The cook looked at Amelia with narrowed eyes but she didn't say anything. She just cleaned off Amelia's arm and dabbed on some sort of stinky ointment. Then she wrapped the burn in a strip of linen and tied the ends to keep it on.

"It's not so bad as it might be," Miss Josephine said finally, "and my ointment should take care of it. Still, you'd better go see Doctor Galt tomorrow and let him have a look see also. He might have some of his fancy London medicine to give you. Now get on with what's left of your chores. It's getting dark and Mr. Pryor said you couldn't go to bed 'till you've done them."

"I can't go see Doctor Galt," Amelia said miserably. "Mr. Pryor burned his book. I've lost his wonderful book and he'll never forgive me. I can't face him again."

Miss Josephine wrinkled up her face and frowned, like she was trying to decide about something. Then she must have made up her mind, for she went over to a shelf in the

She went over to a shelf in the corner

corner. She pulled out something hidden in a bowl, a little bundle wrapped up in a piece of blue and white checked linen cloth.

Silently, she handed it to Amelia.

Puzzled, Amelia took the bundle and unwrapped it. When she saw it was a book, she began to hope. Yes, it was! It was *Domestic Medicine*!

Amazingly, the book was hardly damaged. The outside cover had spots that were dark and sooty, that was all. It seemed that the thick leather cover wouldn't easily catch fire and it must have protected the inside pages.

Looking at the book safe again in her hands, Amelia's mood changed instantly from misery to gladness. She must have saved the book from burning after all when she struggled to pull it out of the fire. All her trouble and pain were worth it.

"Now don't you go telling anyone I gave this to you," Josephine told Amelia sternly. "And Mr. Pryor'd better not find out it's saved. It's lucky I happened to see it this morning before I built up the fire. It was lying there by the side in the ashes."

"Thank you, Miss Josephine," Amelia whispered softly. She felt so much better that she was almost afraid she'd wake up and find she'd only been dreaming.

chapter 17

The next day, Amelia went to see Doctor Galt about her arm. She was afraid to go, but Miss Josephine made her go.

"Don't you worry about Mr. Pryor," she told Amelia, "I'll take care of it."

Amelia took the book back to him as well, with its cover looking sooty and burned, and she told him what had happened.

All the time she explained, Amelia looked down at the floor. She was so sure he'd be mad at her, she was afraid to even look at him. She was astonished and relieved, however, at his reaction.

"I'm sorry for you," he said when she was done, looking very sorry indeed. "It sounds like you've had a hard time of it. Don't worry about the book. I can buff up the leather and it will be fine. But maybe you should let me keep it for a while—not because I care about the book, but for your sake. I expect Mr. Pryor might be extra-vigilant just now and you don't want to get into any more trouble."

Amelia had to admit that sounded like a good idea, so she left *Domestic Medicine* with Doctor Galt. She also thought it might be a good idea to spend the next days concentrating extra hard on her chores.

She was glad that she did, for Mr. Pryor definitely was being, as Doctor Galt said, "extra vigilant." She even thought he'd been going through her few belongings, looking to see if she'd hidden anything away. Sometimes her things didn't seem to be quite the way she'd left them. Luckily, she kept the things she cared about most, like the letter from Doctor Mercer and her mother's locket, safely tucked away in her pocket.

So Amelia worked extra hard at her chores. But still, she didn't work equally hard at everything. She'd do some things as quickly as she could, never mind how well, so she had time to help take care of the horses. She brushed them and fed them and spent a lot of time sweeping and tidying up their stalls and the rest of the stable. John, who was good with the horses but pretty lazy otherwise, thought she was silly to do it.

"There's no point to that," he'd often observe when he found her cleaning up the stable. "Those horses don't care if it's a mess, so long as they're fed and brushed and watered."

Maybe he was right but Amelia didn't care. She wanted the stable to be the way she'd like it to be, if she was one of the horses.

So there she was, sweeping up bits of straw, when the door burst open suddenly and a young girl ran in. The girl was red in the face and breathing hard. She looked as scared as anything.

The girl stood there for a moment trying to catch her breath and then she looked around uncertainly. When she saw Amelia, she looked even more afraid, as if she thought that Amelia might harm her.

Amelia could tell right away that the girl was well-to-do. She wore a gown of lovely green, pink, and white striped silk and her hat was trimmed with matching ribbons. She had silver buckles on her leather shoes, white leather gloves, and little pearl drops on her earlobes.

The frightened stranger was about her own age, thought Amelia, maybe a bit older or younger. But what a world of difference there was between them! She herself was just a poor servant, dressed in old and ragged clothes, while this girl in her fancy clothes was obviously a fine young lady. Why would a fine young lady like her be so frightened?

Amelia put aside the broom and went over to her side.

"Can I help you?" she asked, trying to sound kind and friendly.

"A man is chasing me," the girl said hurriedly, "and I'm afraid of him. Can you hide me?"

Amelia didn't think twice about helping her. She tried to think, what was the best place to hide? In with the horses? No, that wouldn't do. It had to be somewhere the man wouldn't look and besides (Amelia looked again at the fine silk gown) it would be kind of dirty in the stalls with the horses.

What about the loft? You had to climb up a pretty rickety little ladder to get there. It was all right for someone small and light, but the man might not want to climb it, especially if he was big or heavy.

"Up there, quickly!" she whispered to the girl. "Hide yourself in the loft."

No sooner had the girl climbed up and hidden herself when the door burst open and a man strode roughly into the stable. He had a terrible fierce scowl on his face and he looked very odd. His suit was of fine cloth, well made, but it was old, stained, and messy. His waistcoat was buttoned all wrong, one knee of his britches was unbuckled, and his jacket looked like he'd put it on in a hurry.

No wonder the girl was scared of the man, Amelia thought to herself. That man would scare almost anybody.

Hide yourself in the loft

But after living with Mr. Pryor for so long, Amelia wasn't scared very easily.

"I'm looking for a runaway servant!" the strange man told Amelia. "She's a young girl, about your age or a little older. Have you seen her? You'd better tell me! She's stolen her clothes and some gold besides."

Amelia knew right away the man was lying.

"There hasn't been anyone here," she said calmly, and she just kept right on sweeping. Then she gave the man a greedy look and held out her hand. "What does she look like? If it's gold you're seeking, you can afford to pay. For a shilling I'll look out for her."

The man looked around suspiciously with narrowed eyes. He stared especially hard at the ladder. Then he looked at Amelia again as if deciding what to do.

Amelia just stood there with her hand held out for a shilling, trying to look mean and greedy. Finally the man frowned at her, turned away, and left the stable, slamming the door behind him.

Amelia smiled in triumph. The man had believed her!

Then she felt a stab of concern. What if he didn't? What if he was only testing her?

The girl in the loft left her hiding place and looked down, but Amelia gestured urgently that she should stay hidden and out of sight.

Sure enough, an instant later the door opened and the man looked in again. All he saw, though, was Amelia sweeping, just as before. Scowling even more, he left again.

After a while, Amelia opened the stable door and looked outside. She didn't see him anywhere.

"I think he's gone," she called up to the girl. "You can come down now."

Amelia had to laugh when the girl came down from the loft, she looked so comical. She had so many bits of straw sticking out of her hair and on her gown that she looked like a scarecrow. At first the girl looked offended that Amelia was laughing at her, but then she began to laugh at herself also.

Together they got rid of the straw and tidied her up again. She was so thankful for Amelia's help that she tried to give her the hat she was wearing, the one with all the lovely silken ribbons.

"Oh no, I couldn't!" Amelia couldn't help but feel wistful and sad. "He wouldn't let me keep it, anyway."

"Who is 'he'?"

"My Master. My owner. Mr. Pryor."

"Not Mr. Pryor!"

Then the girl seemed to look at her, really look at her, for the very first time. Her eyes lingered on Amelia's bandaged arm and the bruises. "Does he beat you?"

Amelia didn't know how to answer. She felt embarrassed and also afraid. What if this girl knew Mr. Pryor? What if her father was a friend of his?

"He's not so bad," she said quickly. "He has a bit of a temper, that's all. It's just that it was so much better before, in Fredericksburg."

It was amazing how much the girl's face lit up, the instant Amelia mentioned Fredericksburg.

"I have a sister in Fredericksburg!" the girl said excitedly.

"What's her name?" Amelia knew lots of people in Fredericksburg from living there so long. "Maybe I've heard of her."

"I was told that her name was Amelia," the girl said eagerly.

Amelia stared at the girl in surprise.

"Why, that's my name! Amelia! Amelia Watkins."

Amelia looked at the girl more carefully then, her face and her eyes especially. She was sure that she couldn't have ever met her before, and yet somehow this young girl seemed very familiar.

"I don't really know my sister," the strange young girl explained, "because we were separated such a long time ago. Our mother died and our father had to go away, so the Court bound us out as orphans. It all happened here in Williamsburg, but I think that my sister ended up moving to Fredericksburg."

Amelia's eyes widened in surprise. She could hardly believe what she was hearing. This girl's story sounded so much like her own—just like the "once upon a time" story that Mrs. Brown always told her.

"My mother died too," Amelia said slowly, "and my father had to go away. They say he was a sailor. It all happened here in Williamsburg, but then the people I was with, they moved to Fredericksburg. They told me I had a sister too. They said they thought that her name was Amanda."

Amelia hesitated a long, long time, afraid to go on. The other girl was looking at her very strangely. Then Amelia gathered her courage together, as much as she ever had, and asked the question that was burning inside her."

"Is your name Amanda? Could it possibly be you? Could you possibly be my sister?"

The other girl didn't say anything, but tears came to her eyes. One by one, they rolled down her cheeks, softly and silently.

"What have I done?" Amelia thought, pan-ic-stricken. "I must have said something terrible." But then the girl wiped away her tears and smiled.

"I'm Amanda," she said quietly, her voice full of joy. "I'm your sister."

chapter 18

Amelia and Amanda were bursting with so many questions that they hardly knew where to begin, but they barely had time to ask them. All too soon, Amanda suddenly looked worried and pulled out her watch, a pretty little watch that she kept in her pocket.

"Oh dear, I'm so late!" she cried, when she saw what time it was. "I have to go. I'm supposed to meet my father at the tavern. I'm not supposed to be here at all," she went on. "My father—Mr. Lambertson, that is—he doesn't know what I've been doing. All the time I was looking for you, I pretended that I was just shopping."

Amanda gave Amelia a quick little hug and then took off one of her rings, a small silver band with a garnet stone. She pressed it into Amelia's hand. And then she was gone, as if she'd never been there.

For a long time, Amelia just stared into space as if she was in a trance. Had it all been real? Had she really found her sister at last, or had she fallen asleep and just been dreaming?

Then she remembered the silver ring. Yes, there it was, still clutched in her hand. It had all been real! Carefully she put the ring away in her pocket. Then she picked up her broom and went back to sweeping.

The next day, and for days after that, Amelia's feelings were so mixed up that she hardly knew what to do with herself. She felt so happy to have found Amanda at last, but yet so sad to have lost her again. Little by little, though, it all seemed to fade away. Day after day went by, with things just the way they'd always been.

Sometimes Amelia was almost sure that meeting her sister was just a lovely dream. Then she'd feel the ring in her pocket, to remind herself. She really did have a sister and she'd found her at last! But it might as well have been a dream, she thought sadly. She'd found her sister after all this time, but it didn't make any difference at all. Her sister was gone and she was never going to see her again.

Not too much later on, another strange man came to the stable. Amelia was there sweeping up as usual. The stranger poked his head around the door and looked around. When he saw Amelia, he stared at her in a funny sort of way, as if she was some new kind of bug and he was studying her.

At first it gave Amelia quite a fright, the way he just appeared out of nowhere and then stared at her. Then she studied him back and decided that there was nothing to worry about. He seemed a normal sort of man, a proper gentleman, well-dressed and smiling in a friendly, fatherly sort of way. He wasn't at all like that strange, scary man who was chasing Amanda.

"I'm looking for a girl called Amelia. Is that you?" he asked at last.

"Yes, that's me," Amelia answered him cautiously. "I'm Amelia. Can I help you, Sir?"

Then, to her great surprise, he took off his hat and bowed to her. The way he did it, it was as if she was a fine young lady instead of just a servant girl.

"I'm glad to meet you, Amelia," he said. "I'm Mr. Lambertson, Amanda's father."

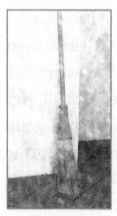

"Mr. Lambertson?!" Amelia was so surprised that you could have knocked her over with a feather. So this was Mr. Lambertson! She hadn't the least idea what to say to him.

"Amanda finally told me about meeting you—finding you, that is," he explained, "so I wanted to come myself to see you. Amanda talks about you all the time," he went on kindly, "and we're all sorry that things have been so hard for you. I wish things hadn't worked out the way they did and that you two couldn't be together."

Amelia found her voice at last.

"Mr. Lambertson, Sir, is Amanda well? Could you tell her I'm thinking of her always?"

"She's thinking of you too, my dear. She's sent you this little letter." He reached in his pocket and pulled out a bit of folded paper.

Amelia put her broom aside, and then timidly took the letter from his hand. Could it be? A letter, for her, from Amanda!

"She said you could read?" Mr. Lambertson asked the question a bit doubtfully.

"Oh, yes!" Amelia took the letter and opened it carefully. She could see Mr. Lambertson was curious to know what the letter said, so she read it out loud to both of them.

"My dearest Amelia," it began, "How very much I miss you! I think about you every day. It's so hard to be so far apart, now that we've finally found each other."

Tears came to Amelia's eyes. Reading the letter, Amanda seemed so near. It was almost as if she could reach out and touch her.

"Even if I got in trouble," Amelia read on, "I just had to tell my mother and father, the Lambertsons, all about you. I told them everything—about how we met, how you looked, about your bruises and the burn and how badly Mr. Pryor is treating you. My father said it was wrong and that he would go to the Court, to see if he could take you instead of Mr. Pryor. Wouldn't that be wonderful! Please have courage and take care. With much love, your sister Amanda."

Mr. Lambertson listened silently to the very end and then he looked at Amelia sadly.

"It's true what she says about going to the Court," he said gravely, "but I'm bound to tell you that the chances are not very great of winning. Still, I'm glad to have met you at last. You're obviously a fine young lady."

And with that, he bowed again and left her.

Amelia ran to the doorway and watched him until he was out of sight. Just before he disappeared around the corner, he looked back and smiled at her.

Amelia read the letter through once again, slowly and more carefully. Going to court! She wondered what would come of it.

Then she remembered how things had been with Penney. Mr. Pryor would be mad and surely he'd win again. She sighed, folded the letter back up, and hid it safely away in her pocket.

chapter 19

Amelia was in the kitchen scrubbing the pots and pans when Mr. Pryor came in, looking as fierce and angry as she'd ever seen him.

"You come with me," he said roughly. He pulled her away from the pots and pans and shoved her out the kitchen door. "I have to go to the Court and they say I have to bring you. That blasted Mr. Lambertson's after me again, trying to steal my servants."

Mr. Pryor stormed right out of the kitchen and kept on walking, holding Amelia by the wrist so she was practically dragged along behind him. It was a freezing cold, snowy day and he hadn't even let her stop to get her cloak. She was so cold, she was shivering.

Once they were inside the courthouse she looked all around, full of curiosity. She'd passed by the courthouse hundreds of times, but she'd never been inside it. Not since that day so long ago that she only barely recalled, when she and Amanda had been separated.

"Where should I sit?" she asked Mr. Pryor timidly.

"Sit? Ha!" Mr. Pryor laughed nastily. "It's bad enough that I'm here at all and had to bring you with me. I'll be hanged if I let you watch things." Still holding her tight by the wrist, he went over to one of the small rooms to the side of the building and pushed her into it. "Don't you dare open this door," he said, and then he slammed it shut behind her.

At first Amelia tried to listen through the door, but it was too thick and heavy. So she sat on a little chair by the window and waited. After a while, the Sherriff came to get her. Then she stood there in front of the Justices while they asked her questions.

It was hard to know what to say, with Mr. Pryor sitting there so close to her and looking like he'd kill her any minute. She told the truth of course, but she answered the questions as quickly as she could, not saying anything more than she had to. Then she was back in the little room, waiting for the rest of it to be over.

She sat there, looking out the window at the gray and wintry sky, and wondered what it would be like to be happy again. Just ordinary happy, nothing special at all. The way she'd been, once upon a time in Fredericksburg.

When the Court ruled for Mr. Pryor, Amelia wasn't surprised. Miss Josephine had warned her beforehand.

"Now don't you go getting your hopes up," she'd said kindly. "Mr. Pryor'll tell them some lies and there's nothing you can do about it. He's a gentleman and you're just a common young girl and a servant."

Surprisingly, though, Mr. Pryor was nicer for a while after the court case. Not really nice, not nice like the Browns had been. Just better than he used to be.

"It won't last, honey," Miss Josephine warned her once again. "The court must've scared him some, so he's being on good behavior. But he'll forget it soon enough and soon he'll be the same as usual."

The change in Mr. Pryor was welcome all the same, for however long it lasted. The mood of the entire household improved. For a few weeks, Amelia felt almost cheerful. She even dared to borrow *Domestic Medicine* again to study it.

Best of all, one especially fine day, she woke up to find a beautiful white stallion in the pasture. From the very first glance, she was pretty sure it was the same horse that she'd fed a carrot to so very long ago, at the September Fair in Fredericksburg.

"Don't you go near that beast," John warned her when he found her standing by the fence with an apple in her

She wondered what it would
be like to be happy again

hand. "His name is Damon but I call him Demon. He's a mean one, to be sure. If you give him a chance, he'll bite your hand off."

If it was really the same horse though, Amelia wasn't scared.

"Who is he? What's he doing here?"

"He belongs to a gentleman from Gloucester. He's visiting here in Williamsburg and we're boarding the horse for him. That horse raced in Fredericksburg, last September Fair, and I hear that he won all the races. Mr. Pryor lost money in that race, on account of betting against him. A lot of money, is what I hear. You were in Fredericksburg then. Maybe you saw him racing?"

"I didn't see the race," Amelia answered, "but I remember the horse. I wonder if he remembers me."

Seeing Damon, she felt like she'd found a long-lost friend. She wasn't afraid and she went right up to him. She held out the apple to him in her hand, hoping she was right that he'd remember her.

At first he looked over toward her with fire in his eyes and she thought she'd made a big mistake. She almost took her hand away again. But she didn't, and a change came over the horse as he got closer. He came up to her and very gently nibbled the apple out of her hand. Then he slightly bowed his head, as if asking her to stroke him.

"Well I'll be!" John had watched the whole thing and he shook his head in amazement. "That horse is bewitched, I swear. I never saw the like of it."

After that, he left the horse alone and made Amelia be the one to take care of him.

A few days later, an even nicer thing happened. Amanda sent her another letter. The Lambertson's coachman delivered it.

"I'm trying to find our father," it said. "Pray I have luck and succeed, for this may solve our problems."

Amelia didn't believe it of course, but it was lovely anyway. It was wonderful just to know she had a sister who cared—that there was one person in the world who really loved her.

chapter 20

As Miss Josephine had predicted, little by little Mr. Pryor changed back to the way he used to be before the lawsuit. As he did, the mood of the household changed as well, until finally it was just as grim as ever.

One day, Mr. Pryor went into Damon's stall. It wasn't a very good idea, because Mr. Pryor didn't like Damon on account of having lost so much money in the race, and Damon didn't like Mr. Pryor either.

The minute Mr. Pryor came near him, Damon started snorting and baring his teeth and huffing. He narrowed his eyes and flattened his ears. John warned Mr. Pryor that he'd better stop, but he didn't. He just kept on coming, but all the time, he was holding up his stick the way he did, like a weapon.

When Mr. Pryor got really close, Damon reared up. He was on his hind legs with his front legs in the air, angry as anything and ready to strike him.

"Watch out!" John shouted. "That horse can kill you!"

This time, Mr. Pryor listened to him. He backed out of the stall and, as he did, he kept striking out with his stick at Damon.

Mostly Mr. Pryor didn't hit anything but air. One time, though, he hit Damon in the foreleg. By then, Damon was so mad that both John and Mr. Pryor were terrified. They left that stable as fast as they could, slamming the door quickly shut behind them.

It was Amelia, coming in later that day, who realized that Damon was limping.

"Something's wrong with Damon," she told John. "He seems to be hurt. What happened?"

John's first answer was to swear like she'd never heard him swear before. Then he apologized for using such language and told her the whole story.

"But now he's hurt," Amelia pointed out. "It might be something bad. You need to do something."

John shook his head.

"I'm not going near that horse again. Not ever. You'll have to take care of it."

"Me? I don't know anything about fixing up horses."

"Well, you'd better find out. It's you or nothing." His tone was so firm, she knew there was no use arguing. She couldn't leave Damon like that, in pain and limping, but what could she do?

Then she remembered Miss Josephine. She could fix people, so what about horses? She went to the kitchen straight away and told her the whole story.

"And John says he won't do anything," Amelia said miserably, when she'd told it all. "And poor Damon's in pain! I can tell Mr. Pryor really hurt him!"

"Don't you worry now," Miss Josephine told Amelia kindly. "Horses aren't so different from people, when you get right down to it. If that horse is still walking around, it's pretty sure nothing's broken. You just go up to him, gentle like, and feel around where it's hurting. Most likely it's a bruise. With all that flailing around with his stick, Mr. Pryor most likely hurt his tendon."

So Amelia did just that. She was a little afraid to get so close to Damon's wounded leg at first, in case it hurt so much that he couldn't help but kick her. She wouldn't have even blamed him. All the time, though, he stood as still as a stone. He just made sad little whinnying noises.

"There's a bump and a cut," she reported back to Miss Josephine, "and the place where he's hurt feels kind of warm. Can you treat him?"

"Oh no, girl," Miss Josephine answered with a chuckle. "You'll not catch me near that horse, poking around where it hurts him. I'm not that crazy."

"But he needs help!" Amelia was near to tears.

"That he does, and you can do it. Now tell me, since you've been studying these things. What's good for broken bones and bruises?"

Amelia thought for a moment.

"Comfrey. Some call it Boneset. It's a healing herb, so that would be best," she said finally.

"Comfrey it is." Miss Josephine smiled. "And it's just your luck that I've got some."

It wasn't really a question of luck, for Miss Josephine had just about every herb that you could ask for. She had

herbs for cooking and herbs for medicine and herbs you could do anything with. She kept some in jars and some in bags or boxes. And some she'd just leave hanging up where they dried, on a rope strung up high in the kitchen.

Now she reached up and pulled down one of the bunches of herbs. She broke off a generous handful of the leaves and handed them to Amelia.

"Here's your comfrey. Now you can use my grinding stone over there"—she pointed to her mortar and pestle—"and you can make yourself a compress."

Amelia remembered how to make compresses. With Miss Josephine watching on, she ground the herb up fine and then added some hot water. She made a kind of paste that she could put on Damon's skin. Then Miss Josephine gave her some long strips of flannel to use as a bandage.

Amelia put the comfrey paste on Damon's leg and carefully wrapped it up with the flannel. Round and round it went, from the knee to the hoof and then back up again. When it was done, she tied it off neatly. Don't wrap it too loose, and not too tight—that's what John had told her, when he finally paid attention to what she was doing.

"And the knot should be in the front," he instructed her, watching her from a safe distance.

"Why in front?"

"Because tying it in the back can put pressure on the tendon and can make it worse," he explained. "Tie it in the front, along the bone where it's nice and solid."

All the time she tended to his leg, Damon stood there patiently and let her do it. It was clear to her that it hurt him to be touched, but he seemed to understand that she was trying to help him. When it was all done, he gave her a little whinny and a nuzzle on the shoulder. From the look in his eyes, she could have sworn he was saying "thank you."

Afterwards, she couldn't help but feel a sense of triumph. She'd finally done it, she'd actually treated someone! True enough, it wasn't exactly how she'd imagined it would be. Her very first patient was a horse, not a person. The way she felt about Damon, though, taking care of him was even better. Now she just had to hope that her treatment would work and his leg would start healing.

chapter 21

After that day, everything went downhill. Amelia's life was as miserable as it had ever been, the whole time since she'd left Fredericksburg. She worked from dawn until late at night, always afraid that, whatever she did, Mr. Pryor would end up punishing her. There wasn't any chance to go see Doctor Galt at all and hardly any time to read *Domestic Medicine*, to sleep, or to talk to Miss Josephine.

The only time Amelia really had to herself was when she was supposed to be taking care of Damon. She pretended it took much longer than it did and everyone (except for Miss Josephine) believed her. It had always taken John a lot of time, when he took care of Damon, because he had to calm him down and be careful not to get kicked or bitten. With Amelia, however, Damon was good as gold, and his leg hardly needed tending. Thanks to her, his tendon was healing splendidly.

Even John was impressed.

"I have to say, I'm surprised," he finally confessed, once it was clear that Damon would completely recover. "I didn't think you could actually do it."

Miss Josephine wasn't surprised. When Amelia told her how the horse was doing, she just smiled and nodded in satisfaction.

It was a fine, bright morning, almost spring, when Mr. Pryor came into the stable unexpectedly. Luckily, at that moment Amelia was brushing Damon down. She thanked her lucky stars that he'd come right then and not just a few moments before, when she'd been reading *Domestic Medicine*.

"You leave that horse and come with me," Mr. Pryor told her sharply. Then, when she didn't move fast enough, he came into Damon's stall to get her.

It wasn't a smart thing to do. After the last time, Damon really hated him. He gave Mr. Pryor an evil look and bared his teeth, and then reared up on his hind legs to strike him. Mr. Pryor barely had time to grab Amelia's arm and drag her out of the stall, before Damon's hooves came crashing down exactly where he'd been standing.

Mr. Pryor marched straight out of the stable and down the street. He kept an iron grip on Amelia's arm and didn't say a word of explanation.

"Where are we going, Mr. Pryor, Sir?" she finally managed to ask when she caught her breath. She was careful to ask softly and timidly.

"Never you mind," he snapped. He walked even faster then and Amelia was running and stumbling, trying to keep up with him.

When they turned onto Duke of Gloucester Street she finally understood, though she could hardly believe it. Could Amanda and the Lambertsons be trying again? Mr. Pryor was taking her to the courthouse.

As they entered the courthouse, Amanda and the Lambertsons were coming in too. Amanda smiled at her, but Amelia could hardly bear to look back at her. How different, how wonderful, things might have been, if only she'd been sent off with her sister to live with the Lambertsons, when the Court sent them off in the first place!

Now here was Amanda at last, her sister and the only family she had, and yet they would always be separated. Amelia was sure that Mr. Pryor would win again. Hadn't he always?

Amelia managed a sad little smile and then looked away, feeling hopeless and miserable. Her eyes were so full of tears that she could barely see. She didn't even notice the stranger who was standing beside Amanda, the man who looked like a sailor.

It was only later, when the Court had begun, that she noticed him. The Sheriff called out "Mr. Watkins, the father of the children, come forward!" and Amelia suddenly realized who it was.

Amanda had done it! She'd found their father! But what was he doing here in court? What would happen now that she'd found him?

"Mr. Watkins," the Chief Justice said, looking down at him solemnly, "what do you say? Do you agree to the Lambertsons adopting your daughter?"

Hearing these words, Amelia's head began to spin. Adopting her? The Lambertsons? She held her breath and looked at her sailor father extra hard. She hadn't seen him in so long, she hardly remembered him.

"Your Honors, Sirs," Mr. Watkins said to the Justices. Then he stopped and looked anxiously over at Mr. Lambertson. Mr. Lambertson gave him an encouraging nod and he went on. "Well, you see, it's like this. I'm a sailor. I love my girls, but I have to be gone—to India, to China, to wherever the winds and waters take me. The girls need to have a real kind of home, Amanda and Amelia."

He looked over at Amelia, standing there by Mr. Pryor's side. As if drawn by some irresistible force, he went over to her. Mr. Pryor tried to get between them, but Mr. Watkins just brushed him aside like a troublesome fly. He put his arms around Amelia and hugged her to him.

"This poor girl, my sweet little Amelia," he went on, and now there were tears in his eyes, "she's been suffering, living with this terrible man, this devil Mr. Pryor. And it's all on account of her not having a proper home, when there's good people who'd like to take proper care of her. These good, kind people," he repeated, and he gestured at the Lambertsons. "So now it's all up to me, whether they do. I guess that's what you're now asking me?"

He stopped and looked up at the Justices. They were hanging on his every word. In answer, the Chief Justice nodded.

"What would you do?" Mr. Watkins went on. "What would any decent father? I love my girls too much not to give them the best I can. Yes, I agree to it all. I'm bound to be off sailing again, wherever the winds may blow, so Amelia and Amanda should be living with Mr. and Mrs. Lambertson."

And with that, the Court's decision was no longer in doubt. Amelia was speechless with wonder.

Then the Court pronounced the verdict and it was done. From this moment on, Amelia would live with the Lambertsons.

The very instant that the Chief Justice finished speaking, Amanda rushed over to Amelia and hugged her and

hugged her. Then Mr. and Mrs. Lambertson came over and hugged them both, and Mr. Watkins hugged everyone. Mr. Pryor stormed out of the courthouse but they never even noticed that he was gone. They were too busy being happy. Amelia was the happiest of all. Now she had a home, a sister, and a family. The dark days of living with Mr. Pryor were gone forever. Her long ordeal was finally over.

The End

Acknowledgments

The author would first and most of all like to gratefully acknowledge Abby and Emma Hogan, not only for being such excellent models for Amelia and Amanda, but also for their lively interest and important feedback (along with that of their younger brother Sam). I am grateful also to my reenactor friends who make such splendid 18th century characters—Chuck Aldrich, Dory Cunningham, Buzz Mooney, and Cindy Palmer, with special thanks to Signora Bella (Jody Ellis, www.signorabella.com), who is the real-life "Signora La Rosa." Thanks to Ann Gates for her support, encouragement, and editorial assistance; to test-readers Cindy Palmer and Prem Shakti for their for their useful suggestions; to Kari LaBell for sharing her expertise on herbs and horses; and to Stephanie Anderson of Jera Publishing and David Kosar for their assistance with design and illustrations. Thanks to Kim Walters (www.kwaltersatthesignofthegrayhorse.com) for providing Amelia's locket and Amanda's ring; to John Bortniak for the quill-penned letter; to Linda Zeigler, colonial food-ways expert, for her wonderful kitchen fireplace; and to Colonial Williamsburg and the other historic sites that have generously shared their expertise and are pictured in various illustrations: Belair Mansion in Bowie, Maryland; Claude Moore Farm in McLean, Virginia; Gunston Hall (home of George Mason) in Lorton, Virginia; the Historic Fredericksburg Foundation and the Hugh Mercer Apothecary Shop in Fredericksburg, Virginia; Historic Londontown and Gardens in Edgewater, Maryland; Mount Harmon Plantation in Earleville, Maryland; and the Stabler-Leadbeater Apothecary Shop in Alexandria, Virginia. Last (but far from least), I could never have done this were it not for my dear husband Ted Borek and his constant loving support and patience.

It has been suggested that this book and *Amanda's Secret* would be more useful for school reading credit if there were accompanying study questions and these are now in progress. Look for them at www.Shrewsburypress.com.

CPSIA information can be obtained at www.ICGtesting.com
Printed in the USA
BVOW11s0928181115

427564BV00003B/6/P